Mountain Mishap

by

Janice Cole Hopkins

Other Books by Janice Cole Hopkins

The Appalachian Roots series

Cleared for Planting – book one
Sown in Dark Soil – book two
Uprooted by War – book three
Transplanted to Red Clay – book four

(Slight connection but not a series or sequel)

When Winter Is Past
With Summer's Songs

The Farmers trilogy

Promise – book one
Peace – book two
Pardon – book three

For behold, the Lord cometh forth out of his place, and will come down, and tread upon the high places of the earth.

Micah 1:3

Chapter One: The Appalachians

Western Wilkes County, July 4, 1851

Levi West stopped his horse and dismounted. The animal needed a break, and the breathtaking view ahead needed more reflection. His eyes roamed over the majestic cliffs. They seemed to lift his spirits to high places. Good. He needed that.

The air had already turned cooler and fresher smelling. He breathed in deeply and felt his body relax. He felt secluded here, but not alone. No, he felt closer to God than ever before. At this high elevation, it seemed as if he'd stepped up toward heaven. He laughed at himself, but it felt good to laugh again. He couldn't remember the last time he'd managed more than a weak smile.

He remembered the scattered decorations he'd seen in Wilkesboro to observe Independence Day. Wilkesboro had been a nice town, and he'd considered settling there but had decided against it. He had his mind set on living up in the mountains, away from so many people. He had an older brother living there, and Noah had written that Levi would be welcome anytime.

"Come on, Jack." He gave the reins a tug as he started walking. The grade had gotten steeper, and Jack had already brought him a long ways. It would be good for him to walk a while and get used to the steep inclines and thinner air.

They got to the top of one of many inclines when the sun looked down from directly overhead. Levi stopped near a small creek, gave Jack a drink, and sat down to eat the ham biscuits he'd packed that morning. The climb had worn him out.

They made it to where the elevation smoothed out just as a summer storm hit. Levi pulled out his poncho, tucked his head down as much as possible, and continued on. The thunder sounded different than any he'd ever heard before. It rumbled and reverberated as if it were a giant metallic ball ricocheting between the peaks.

The rain had stopped and the sky had cleared by the time he rode Jack into the small mountain town Noah had told him about. His brother said that when he got to Boone he wouldn't have but about a half a day's ride left. Since he didn't have half a day left before nightfall, he decided he'd stay put for the night and have plenty of time to get there sometime tomorrow. The gray-purple tones of dusk had him looking up again. Something about this place touched his heart and soul.

The next morning Levi went to the general store and bought a few things he thought he might need soon. He didn't expect his brother came into town often. He also bought some eggs and bacon to cook for a late breakfast. That should hold him until he got to Noah's cabin.

"Yeah, I know Noah West," the store clerk said. "He seems to be a good man. Lives over toward Tennessee. You know he got married?"

"Yes, he told me in his letter, but I've never met her."

"You have directions to his place?"

"I do. I think I can find it. At least, I've got all day to try."

"Well, you came at a good time. July is the only month not even the old-timers have heard of it snowing."

"I heard the winters are rough, but I like snow. Like to hunt in it."

The man laughed. "You'll likely be sick of snow and cold weather before the first winter is over, but I wish you luck."

Levi felt like telling him a man didn't need luck when he had the Lord to bless him, but he didn't want to sound sanctimonious, since he didn't feel better than any man. The way he saw it, we all have our own set of sins, but grace would cover them if we asked.

He took his time getting to his brother's place, for he felt no need to hurry. If he didn't get there today, he'd get there tomorrow or the next day. He took time to enjoy the scenery, some of the prettiest he'd ever seen in his life. Strange, but in some mysterious way, he felt like he'd come home. Yet, he'd never been farther west than Salisbury before now, and he and Noah had never been particularly close.

The sun showed mid-afternoon when Levi picked his way between trees to come to the cabin. It looked solid but small. He hoped he wouldn't inconvenience Noah and Daisy too much.

He saw Noah out back in the garden, so he dismounted and led his horse in that direction. Noah dropped his hoe and came to meet him.

"Howdy, brother."

When he put out his hand, Noah encased it with both of his. "Glad you finally made it, Levi. I didn't know if you'd ever come or not."

"I didn't write, because I figured I'd get here before the letter would."

"Getting mail in and out of here is quite a feat. That's why you haven't heard from me much. There's spotty service to the general store in Boone, but I don't get in there often. But come in the house. I want you to meet Daisy."

Daisy turned out to be a sturdy looking woman with reddish, brown hair. She looked Levi over from head to toe when Noah introduced them. He must have passed inspection, because she gave him a warm smile that reached her eyes and make them sparkle.

"Welcome, Levi. I hope I can call you 'Levi.'"

He nodded, unsure of what her friendliness might mean, but then he scolded himself. He needed to leave his recent experiences down the mountain, and not let them taint the present. He came here for new surroundings and a new beginning.

"Supper will be ready in about two hours. Would you like something to eat or drink before then?"

"Thank you, no. I'll just go take care of my horse and maybe get a drink of water from that springhouse I saw out back."

She nodded and turned back to her work. Regardless of his resolve to leave the past behind, it made him feel better that Daisy turned away. He'd hate to have to leave his brother's after just getting here.

He took Jack to the log barn, brushed him down, and put him in a stall with feed and water. When he went to the springhouse for some water, Noah followed. "So, tell me. What brings you here now? I know it has to be more than just wanting to pay me a visit."

Levi sucked in his breath. He had hoped he would get by without talking about it. Well, he'd begin with telling as little as possible, but if he remembered right, Noah had always been the inquisitive type. "When Mama and Papa died of the fever, I had to sell the farm to pay off the debts. There was nothing left for me there."

"I didn't know he'd left things in that bad a shape."

"Yeah, well, he never cared that much about farming. He was a preacher at heart, but the farm should have been our livelihood and made up for the small pittance the church could pay. However, the records showed that he used farm funds to keep up the church."

Noah took the gourd dipper down and handed Levi some water. "I'm sorry about that, but something tells me you wouldn't have left the flatlands for that reason alone. You could always have found a job there. I can't believe you left T. J. You and he have been almost inseparable since you were out of diapers."

"Things change."

Noah tilted his head to stare at Levi. "If things change that much between two close friends, there must be a woman involved."

Levi winced. So much for keeping secrets. A shiver ran down his back, and he didn't know if it came from the memories or the coolness in the springhouse. He stepped outside and sat down on the rough bench against the wall.

Noah joined him. "You'll feel better once you get it off your chest."

He didn't think so, but he knew Noah wouldn't relent. "T. J. became enthralled with Leanore Sharpe."

"The doctor's daughter?"

"Yes. He had a ring in his pocket planning to propose. However, she came to see me at the farm and pretty much threw herself at me. She said she'd allowed the wrong man to court her, and she wanted me. When I just stood in shock, she put her arms around me and began to kiss me. T. J. walked up and saw us in the barn. I thought he was going to kill me by the look on his face, but he just turned and stomped away. I tried to tell him what had happened, but he wouldn't listen, wouldn't see me. I wrote him a note but he tore it up. So, I packed up and came here. Both of us didn't need to be in the same town, and I hoped, if I left, he and Leanore would work things out."

"Did you like her?"

"Not at all. Actually, I couldn't understand what T. J. saw in her. She's too haughty and demanding for me."

Noah shook his head. "You always did attract the girls. It's your looks, I guess. You turned out to be the best looking one of us."

"If that's true, it's a curse and not a blessing."

"One day you'll meet a woman who will make you change your mind."

Truth be told, Levi would like to have a family, but he didn't want to settle for just any wife. He wanted a woman who loved the Lord as much as he did. He wanted one who didn't think so highly of herself that she thought everyone needed to cater to her, who wasn't so selfish and self-centered. He looked around him. And, he needed one who didn't shy away from hard work. All the women he'd met so far fell short.

Noah slapped him on the back. "Well, come on, little brother. The day's a-wasting, and there's work to be done."

Good. Some hard work might get his mind off the past and back on these beautiful mountains. God had brought him here for a purpose. He believed that.

They hadn't worked in the garden long when Daisy called them to supper. She'd cooked a chicken stew.

"Since I have the garden in and we don't hunt in the summer months, I thought you and I would build another room on the back. That way, you'll have a bedroom." Noah didn't look up from his plate.

Levi looked around the one-room cabin. They'd hung a couple of quilts for partitions around the bed. It looked like Noah had built a cot for him and placed it on the opposite wall. "That sounds good. With both of us working it shouldn't take long."

"My sister is talking about coming to stay the winter with us, too. I come from a big family over near Trade, Tennessee. There're two boys and six of us girls. I'm the oldest, and Violet is almost two years younger. How old are you, Levi?"

"I'll be twenty-six come my next birthday." Could she be any more obvious? He didn't need a matchmaker. "I hope I'm not imposing."

"Nonsense. We can always make room for one more. I'm used to a crowd."

"I'm not interested in meeting any women right now, so please don't try to arrange that."

Daisy's smile fell. "Violet is coming to see me, and to create a little more space for the others when they have to be cooped up in the bad weather that comes with winter here."

Maybe he'd been too straightforward but better to make things clear at the very beginning so there'd be no misunderstandings.

As the days passed, Levi worked hard on the new room. He'd never lived in such close quarters before, and the occasional rustling covers and squeaks from the bed bothered him. But he'd come up with a solution of sorts.

He had started getting up at the first break of day and taking his Bible outside. He'd found an Indian trail that led around the mountain and to a great spot to have his devotion. He sat on a large rock, surrounded by mountains and overlooking a lovely valley. He began his day with Bible study, prayer, and glorifying God. If he felt like it, he could sing his heart out with hymns he remembered and not worry about making anyone cringe.

It also gave Noah and Daisy some time alone. When he got back to the house, he milked the cow, gathered the eggs, and went in for breakfast. After breakfast, he and his brother worked on the addition, in the garden, or with the animals. On Sunday afternoons they often went fishing, although getting to a stream large enough to fish in took a while.

Levi hated it that they couldn't get to a church service on Sundays. He held a service of sorts for the three of them in the house, but it would have been better to hear a preacher. Levi's faith didn't grow as much when he did it himself. He liked to hear others' ideas.

The summer warmth passed more quickly here than down the mountain, but the vibrant autumn colors on the leaves made Levi rejoice. He'd never seen such glory. When he sat on his rock for his devotion, the view might be shrouded in fog. But when the sun came out and wrapped its light around the day, the colors nearly stole his breath away. How could anyone see God's creation and not believe?

Fall also meant Levi could begin hunting, and he loved to hunt. He didn't enjoy the kill as much as he liked trekking through the woods or sitting in a tree, but they could use the extra meat, so he would hunt in earnest. He set the rabbit gums for Noah and shot a deer his first time out. The forest seemed fuller of wildlife here than back home. The more he saw of the place, the more he appreciated its rugged beauty and bounty.

Fall brought a lot of hard work, too. He helped Noah get in the harvest and kill a hog. They'd cut enough firewood to last them three or four years at home, but Noah said they'd need to cut more on the warmer days of winter. And they repaired and got the outbuildings ready for winter.

Violet came the first of October. She had blazing red hair and pale blue eyes. He could see a resemblance between the sisters, but Daisy's hair had more brown in it, and Violet had finer bones and a more attractive face. Levi guessed most people would call her pretty, but he felt no attraction.

Had Leanore tainted him against all women? He had certainly struggled to forgive her for causing such a rift with T. J. He'd had to pray for God's Spirit to guide him, because he hadn't been capable of forgiving her on his own.

He'd given Violet the bedroom and moved back to the cot. He figured women needed more privacy than a man did, but he missed having a room of his own.

Violet's eyes told him of her interest, and that made him more cautious. He started going hunting and checking the rabbit gums more often. He'd thought about building some more of the wooden traps. He could easily make the simple, long box with a notched stick to spring the door. However, they were catching plenty of rabbits in the ones he'd set, so he decided new ones weren't needed.

"Rose was excited to be the oldest girl left at home for a while," Violet told Daisy at the table one morning.

"Are all your sisters named after a flower?" Levi asked.

Violet giggled. "Just the first three, because those flowers were Mama's favorites, although I do wish she'd kept it up. The others could have been Pansy, Petunia, Dahlia, Camilla, Iris, Lily, or even Lilac. Why, the possibilities are almost endless."

"Maybe we can use some of those names when we have children," Daisy added.

"I'm hoping for some boys." Noah looked serious. "And I don't want them to have any of those flower names."

Violet giggled again. "Maybe we could name them Leif, Ash, Woody, or Oleander, and I think even Heath is a plant name."

Levi almost shook his head. Silly woman. But he put his attention on his plate instead.

"I guess Noah and I will be choosing one of those names come about April or May."

Levi jerked his head up. Had Daisy just said what he thought she had?

She'd blushed a dark pink. "You're going to be an uncle, Levi, and Violet will be an aunt."

"I thought we might fix a sleeping loft this summer for the little ones as they get older," Noah told them.

Levi nodded, trying to ascertain what this new revelation would mean for him. Maybe he should consider Violet. He knew it wouldn't take much courting to get her to marry him, and he felt sure Noah would give him some land where he could build his own cabin. In fact, his brother would help him build it.

He looked at Violet. A man could do worse, but, for some reason, his heart wanted to hold out for more.

Chapter Two: Charleston Orphan

Charleston, South Carolina, May 1852

Anna Allen's pace slowed to that of a sloth as she neared Mrs. Bull's office. She'd walked much faster this morning when she'd gone around the orphan house to see it for the last time. Now she felt as if she walked to the gallows instead of the man she could marry, although she'd never set eyes on him before.

She looked around, stalling. This had been the only home she remembered well. A neighbor had brought her here when her parents had both died of a summer fever. It hadn't been an easy life, but she'd received a good education and had been taught all the skills she'd need to take care of a household.

She moved to the door, but paused before knocking, remembering what Mrs. Bull had told her yesterday. "Anna, I had hoped that you could move on to teachers' training. You're one of my most accomplished students, but the teachers' training school doesn't accept many, and they're already filled for this year. As you know, the apprenticeships and indentures have practically dried up, and I always worry about the girls I indentured anyway. The best option for you is to be married. I have a young man coming by tomorrow and he wants to look over those who are sixteen and older in order to choose his wife. As pretty as you are, I think there's a good chance you'll be chosen. I really do think this will be your best option, since you're eighteen and can't stay here any longer."

"Couldn't I stay here and help with the younger children?"

Mrs. Bull looked sympathetic. "You know the older orphans do that. We never have enough food as it is, so we can't keep on extra mouths to feed. I'm sorry, but I'll pray for a good situation for you."

Anna tried not to notice the other girls who'd already gone into the room earlier, one at a time. She hadn't seen all of them.

She tried to swallow down the lump in her throat as she knocked on the door. When she entered, two men stood. Both had light brown hair and hazel eyes, although the older man's hair looked darker and his eyes more golden, and the younger man stood a few inches taller, giving him a lanky appearance.

"Mr. Ramsey, I'd like to introduce you to the last of our older girls. This is Anna Allen. Anna, this is Elbert Ramsey and his father, Hiram. They have a cabin in the Appalachian mountains."

Anna lowered her eyes. "Pleased to meet you both."

Elbert's eyes nearly glowed with excitement when she looked back up. "How old are you, Miss Allen?"

"Eighteen, sir."

"Call me Elbert," he smiled. "You can save the sirs fer Pa thar."

"And I take hit you can read and write?" the older man asked. Although Elbert looked as if he'd cleaned up some, his father didn't.

"Yes, sir."

"And you can cook and do such chores?"

"I assure you, Mr. Ramsey, that our girls are well trained." Mrs. Bull sounded almost insulted.

Elbert cut in. "I'll take this one if'n she'll have me."

Mrs. Bull looked at Anna after Elbert's declaration. She almost felt as if they'd put her on the auction block. "C-c-could we walk outside? J-just the two of us f-for a moment?"

Mrs. Bull's face softened. "Under the circumstances, I think that will be all right. I understand this is an overwhelming decision, Anna. I'll be praying for you." She turned to Mr. Ramsey. "In the meantime, let me show you our facility, Mr. Ramsey, and you'll see for yourself what a fine establishment the Charleston Orphan House is."

Anna led Elbert outside toward the garden. At the orphan house, that meant a vegetable garden.

"I know you must have some questions." Elbert took her hand.

She wanted to pull it away, but she didn't. She'd needed to get used to his touch if she agreed to be his wife.

"We live in a log cabin on a wooded mountain. We hain't got no close neighbors. I guess ar cabin is small by Eastern standards, but hit serves ar purpose. Pa and me built an extra bedroom on hit before we come, so me and my wife could have some privacy."

"You knew you were coming to find a wife then?"

"Yeah. Pa comes to Charleston about ever' ten years or so to take keer of some business and git some thangs he can't git in Boone or Trade. Those are the two closest towns. We live between 'em. This year he tells me hit might be a good time to look to gettin' me a woman. You see thar ain't many sangle women in the mountains, and I don't have no time for courtin' no how."

"Just you and your father live in the cabin?"

"Yeah. Ma died a few years back, and several babies died at birth. I had a sister that lived to be eight, but she died with the croup." He looked at her body. "I hope you want to have children."

"I do." She'd always dreamed of a family of her own, but she'd never imagined it starting this way.

"I'll see to your needs, and try my best to provide for you. Hit might be a hard life in the mountains, but hit can be a good life. I've never seed a purtier place.

Although hit's different than here, I thank you'll fit in jus' fine." He grinned. "You're a purty little thang, too."

"Is that why you picked me, because you liked the way I looked?"

"That wuz part of hit. There's somethang about you that reached right out and tugged at my heart, and I said to myself, "This here's the one. None of the other five did that."

"Are you a Christian man?"

"Well, I believe in God, and I've been baptized. Ma saw to that one day when a preacher man got lost and ended up at the farm. However, we hain't got no church close enough to go to."

"Do you read your Bible or hold your own services on Sunday?"

He looked away. "I can't read nor write, but you can take that up if'n you'd like." He gave her hand a little squeeze. "You ready to go back in now?"

She nodded and gave Elbert a thorough examination as they returned. He stood a few inches taller than her five-foot, five inches. He had light brown hair, and a bushy beard that needed trimming. His hazel eyes didn't appear unkind, but she'd seen no special warmth in them either. At least he looked clean, and she could tell he had on a new set of clothes, bought for their practicality.

As they entered the large building that took up nearly a whole city block, Anna realized no amount of questions she might ask today would give the answers she wanted. Only time would. She sighed. She also realized she had few options. She'd just have to trust in God for the outcome.

"You got any idee what your choice is gonna be?" Elbert asked as they neared Mrs. Bull's office door.

"I've decided to accept your kind offer of marriage."

Mrs. Bull arranged for the wedding to take place in the sitting room. Anna put on her best dress, a blue calico cotton trimmed with white lace she'd made herself. The other girls said it matched her blue eyes and made her look divine. Some of them helped put her blonde hair up at the back of her head. Mrs. Bull gave her some hair pins for a wedding present and let her borrow a pair of white gloves.

"I can't believe you're getting married today," Lucy said. "It's so romantic."

Anna couldn't believe it either, but she didn't know about the romantic part. She hoped she would look back on it and think so, because of the way her husband treated her, but she had her doubts. Something told her that Elbert wouldn't be the romantic sort.

That was confirmed when he and his father walked into the sitting room wearing the same clothes they'd worn earlier. Elbert hadn't even brought her a single flower, although they bloomed everywhere in Charleston in May. A man in a suit, obviously the preacher, followed them.

In almost no time, they'd said their vows, and the simple service ended. She'd just become Mrs. Elbert Ramsey.

"What's your plans, Mr. Ramsey?" she heard Mrs. Bull ask.

"Well I guess hit's too late in the day to start out now. I reckon we'll stick around here and git an early start in the mornin'. We've got a room at a boardin' house."

"Well Anna's things are all packed." She walked over and kissed Anna's cheek in a rare show of affection. "I wish you all the happiness in the world."

"Thank you ma'am, for all you and orphan house has done for me."

"I hate to see you go. You're one of the best residents we've ever had." Did the woman regret pushing Anna to marry Elbert? Too late now.

Although Anna wouldn't be able to use her extensive academic education in the mountains, she'd been taught housekeeping skills that would come in handy. And she'd be able to give her children a good education. Yes, she hoped for a good life.

The boarding house looked run-down, attesting to the fact that the Ramseys didn't have much money. But the inside of the dwelling looked clean, and Anna relaxed. She had never been used to fancy furnishings anyway.

"I'll get us another room," Elbert said.

"What fer?" Mr. Ramsey sounded almost angry.

"Fer me and Anna. Fer our wedding night."

"Won't be anythang I hain't seen, and I know you ain't shy around me."

Anna knew her face must be beet-red, and she wanted to die right there. She looked for a chair, not sure how much longer her legs would hold her.

Elbert must have noticed her state, because he reached over and took her arm. "I figure some of that money we saved for the trip is mine, Pa. I helped earn hit. I'm goin' to have a separate room for tonight where my new bride won't be skeered to death. What you're suggestin' ain't even decent."

"Humph! You know I sleep like the dead, but have hit your way. You take the room. I'll go bed down in the stable and be back here with the wagon at daybreak. You have the woman who runs this place here to pack us some breakfast. I'll bring vittles for the other meals."

"Thanks, Pa."

Mr. Ramsey turned to Anna. "I'm givin' in this one time, and only this one time. Don't get used to being coddled, hear me."

Anna felt tears spring to her eyes. Did the man not like her?

"Hit wuzn't her, Pa. This is my idee."

Elbert moved his arm from her elbow to her waist as they started to their room. "Don't worry, honey. We'll have our own bedroom when we get home."

She sniffed to clear her voice. "I'm glad you thought to build it."

Anna didn't know what to think of her first night with her husband. Thanks to a brief lecture from Mrs. Bull, she knew some of what to expect, but everything seemed to happen quickly. Elbert kissed her, fondled her, and they were intimate. Then, he turned over and went to sleep.

Did she have some unrealistic, fairytale idea of marriage? She'd read enough literature to think she should enjoy some part of this. Had she been wrong? Is this what Mrs. Bull meant by "wifely duty?"

Even the next morning, Elbert seemed satisfied, but he said nothing, and he didn't kiss her again. As they gathered their things and went out the door, he did whisper, "I'd like to have took more time in the room this mornin', but, if'n I know Pa, he'll be here waitin' on us. I didn't want him to try to come bargin' into the room or somethang. He's not known fer his patience."

They picked up a sack of food from the kitchen, and found Mr. Ramsey sitting out front in the wagon just as Elbert had guessed. "'Bout time you git here."

The wagon only had the one seat, and with a load in the back, Anna had no choice but to climb in beside Mr. Ramsey. Sandwiched between the two men, this would be a long trip.

"Woman, I thought you could cook!" Mr. Ramsey spewed the words in disgust.

Anna had never cooked on a campfire before, and the pot sat in the flame instead of being hung on the fireplace hook. The ham turned out okay, but the grits had lumped up some. The cornbread fritters had turned out all right, too.

She looked at Elbert, trying to judge his reaction. He must have thought she expected him to say something to his father on her behalf. "Aw, Pa. This is all new to her. Give her some time and she'll git the hang of hit. Hit's not that bad." He took another bite of his grits to prove his point.

"I told her jus' to fix ham and grits fer supper, thankin' that would be easy on her." Mr. Ramsey didn't want to let it drop. "You jus' picked her fer her looks, didn't you, son? Well, looks don't git the work done. You shoulda picked that big-boned girl that come in first."

Elbert stiffened. "You said I could do the pickin', and I did. If'n you wanted the big-boned woman, maybe you should have purposed to her yourself."

Mr. Ramsey's fist shot out so fast neither she nor Elbert saw it coming. Elbert staggered back from the blow, but he didn't fall, although his plate went flying through the air with food scattering everywhere.

Anna knew her eyes must have been as big as saucers. What had she gotten herself into?

"Don't you back-talk me, boy. You know I ain't goin' put up with no sassin'." Mr. Ramsey took his plate and stomped off to the other side of the wagon.

Elbert tried to wipe the blood from the corner of his mouth, and his cheek had already started to swell.

Anna jumped up. "Here, sit down, Elbert. I'll get a cloth and some water and clean you up." He obeyed without a word.

"I'm sorry," she whispered, as she washed the blood away and applied the cool cloth to his cheek. "I didn't mean to cause trouble."

"You didn't cause hit. Nothin' seems to suit Pa lately. I thank he'll be better once we git back to the hills. I'll jus' try to 'bide my tongue better 'til then. I knowed I'd said too much as soon as hit left my mouth." His eyes softened when he looked at her. "I didn't want no big-boned woman. I wanted you."

She gave him a weak smile. "Lendie, the big-boned girl, is about as clumsy as they come. I doubt if she'd have suited your father either."

He smiled as much as his cracked lip would let him. "No, she wouldn't, and she sure wouldn't have suited me."

Anna wanted to ask him if she suited him, but she didn't. Better not to go fishing for compliments. Elbert might not be the husband of her dreams, but he didn't appear to be as hard or as demanding as his father, and she should be grateful for that. However, she had to live around both men.

Anna and Elbert bedded down on the ground on one side of the wagon. "This way, we can scoot under the wagon if hit rains," Elbert told her.

If it rained hard, they'd still get soaked from water running under the wagon, but she said nothing. With the back full of supplies, they'd have little choice.

Mr. Ramsey bedded down out in the open on the other side of the fire pit. At least he seemed willing to give her and Elbert some space. Or maybe he just wanted to get as far away from Anna as he could and still be in camp.

"Here." Mr. Ramsey shoved a loaf of bread into her hands the next morning. "I bought this in Charleston. Slice hit up and fix some bacon and eggs for breakfast. Fry up enough bacon to put between slices of bread, and we'll have that for dinner."

"Yes, sir."

"I'll get the eggs," Elbert told her. "Pa stored them in the flour and sugar to keep them from breaking."

Anna took care not to mess up anything for breakfast. "See," Elbert told his father. "I told you she's a fast learner."

"'Bout time she put something decent to eat in front of me."

Anna looked away, hoping to ignore the man. This was only the second meal she'd cooked without some others helping.

.

The days proceeded in much the same way. Mr. Ramsey didn't say much, but what he did say came out sharp and cutting. The man seemed mad at the world, but Anna couldn't figure out why.

Elbert wasn't attentive, but neither did he berate her like his father. He didn't seem dissatisfied with her, but she got the feeling that if he ever had to choose between her and his father, he'd choose his father. Although her husband didn't like the way his father treated Anna, the man still had Elbert's loyalty.

Chapter Three: Babies

Noah seemed as nervous as a mosquito in a bat cave. He'd tried to work in the barn but ended up pacing back and forth around the back door to the cabin.

Daisy's mother had come to help with the birthing, and Levi had hoped Violet would go back home for a spell to help with the household, but she didn't. They both stayed, putting a strain on the small cabin. Violet and Mrs. Greer both stayed in the bedroom.

"What's taking so long," Noah mumbled. "I sure hope nothing's wrong."

Levi swiped his hand through his dark hair. If he hadn't been afraid Noah might need him, he'd have gone out in the woods this morning until the crisis passed. He picked up a hoe and contemplated going to the garden and cutting some rows to plant the corn. Noah thought the danger of frost would be gone by the time the corn shoots poked out of the ground. But maybe he should stay near Noah for now.

This sure had been a rough winter, although Noah said it had been milder than some. Levi had never felt such cold. The wind had thrown thousands of icy daggers straight through him, stripping his clothes and freezing him to the core.

He'd never seen so much snow either. At one time, they had over two feet in one snowfall, and the wind caused drifts higher than his head. Sometimes, one snowfall followed another with none of them melting.

He discovered the mountains took on another kind of beauty in the snow. However, he didn't venture to his rock in the snowstorms or for his devotions on a regular basis. He didn't go out as much in the winter at all, although he tried to check his rabbit traps at least twice a week and go hunting as much as possible.

Staying inside had meant he'd been in Violet's company more. He got tired of her trying to engage him in conversation, which meant endless chatter of little substance. Neither she nor Daisy had any education. If he could have discussed books or even his faith, it would have been more satisfying. But not being able to read meant her family had heard little of the Bible, especially since they never went to a church service. He thought spring would never come, but it finally had.

"I hear a baby's cry." Noah sounded both excited and anxious. "You think it's all right for me to go in now?"

"Mrs. Greer said she'd send for you when you could go in, so you'd better wait."

He nodded and resumed pacing. The door opened up, and Violet stood back to let Noah in. "It's a girl. Go on and see her."

Violet came over to Levi. "Our niece is just the cutest little thing. Her hair's a reddish blonde right now, but Mama says it will likely darken."

Levi didn't know how to talk about babies. "Is Daisy all right?"

"My, yes. She's just tired and sore, but she's just fine. Come on. You need to see the baby."

Levi obediently followed her. He'd have his look and then maybe he could spend some time in the woods until near suppertime.

No one got a full night's sleep with the baby in the house. For such a tiny thing, Iris developed a powerful set of lungs fast.

Mrs. Greer went home a few days after her birth, but Violet stayed. Maybe helping care for the baby would divert her attention. A man could hope.

The trip turned out to be longer and more grueling than Anna had imagined. Mr. Ramsey's mood hadn't improved any, and she hoped Elbert was right and he'd lose some of his surliness when they got to the cabin.

When the first of the mountains came into view, the scene touched a place deep within her. The beauty only intensified the farther west they traveled.

"Whatsya lookin' at, girl?" Mr. Ramsey asked. "Hain't you ever seed a mountain before?"

No, sir. I've lived in Charleston all of my life."

"You hain't seen nothin' yet. Has she Pa?"

Mr. Ramsey didn't answer. "I'll be glad to git home," he said instead. "This might be the last time I make this trip."

Anna looked at the man, trying to determine his age but afraid to ask. She'd guess him to be in his early sixties, but he could be younger or older. Elbert had told her he was twenty-nine.

They drove through the town of Boone but didn't stop. Mr. Ramsey couldn't wait to get home and hoped to make it in time to unpack the wagon before nightfall.

When they turned to go to the cabin, Anna couldn't see a road or even a path, but Mr. Ramsey seemed to know which way to go to weave them through the trees.

When the cabin came into sight, Anna tried to hide her disappointment. Besides being small, the cabin looked old and in disrepair.

"Looks like we musta had some storms." Mr. Ramsey looked around the property. "The cabin and the barn needs rechinkin', and the garden has more weeds than anythang else. I knowed hit probably would. Ya'll better sleep good tonight, 'cause come tomorrow all three of us has a ton of work to do."

Anna already felt bone-weary from the trip, but she refused to complain. She'd work just as hard as these men and show Mr. Ramsey that Elbert hadn't made a mistake in choosing her to be his wife. This was her lot now, and she might as well make the best of things. They could be a whole lot worse. She could be married to someone like Mr. Ramsey.

For the rest of the week, Anna worked harder than she'd ever worked in her life, and she'd been used to hard work at the orphan house. Elbert appeared as tired as her every night when they fell into bed.

She not only worked with the men, but she also cooked all the meals. The cabin only had one large, rock fireplace, but it had all the necessities to hang pots or to set them on spiders.

Despite staying so busy, however, it seemed strange not to have an abundance of people around her. She'd had the adults and children from the orphan house around her for so long that it felt almost lonely with just Elbert and Mr. Ramsey, especially since they didn't give her much attention.

"We should finish up weedin' the garden today, and, since we've finished repairin' the chinking on the cabin, we can begin on the barn." Mr. Ramsey talked through his large bite of pancakes.

"But today's Sunday." Anna had held her tongue around Mr. Ramsey all week, but she didn't want to be working so hard on the Lord's Day.

Mr. Ramsey paused and gave her a cutting stare. "And?"

"I only do the necessary tasks on Sunday, since the Bible says it's to be a day of rest."

"I knowed you wuz on the lazy side. You'll do what I tell you."

"Mr. Ramsey, please. I've worked hard this week, and I try to go by what the Bible says."

"She's right, Pa. I remember Ma sayin' the same thang. Hit won't hurt none to take a break fer today. That way we can work all the harder tomorrow."

"Now, she's got you wantin' to shirk your duties." Mr. Ramsey went back to eating, but he didn't say anything else about them continuing to work.

"I'm going to read from my mama's Bible and have a prayer for my Sunday service. Do you want to join me?" Anna asked after breakfast.

"I'd like to hear you read," Elbert said.

Mr. Ramsey looked torn between wanting to hear what she read and not wanting to appear to. "Thar's milkin' to be done, eggs to be gathered, and hogs to be slopped."

"I'm going to clean the kitchen and make the beds first. I expect we'll finish up about the same time."

He nodded, and he and Elbert went outside. Anna breathed a sigh of relief. She felt that she'd won a small victory for the first time.

Elbert listened more attentively than Mr. Ramsey did. The older man closed his eyes much of the time Anna prayed and read, but she had a feeling he paid more attention than it appeared.

"You read good," Elbert said when she'd finished. She smiled her thank you. Her husband rarely gave her any kind of compliment, and she appreciated that he'd enjoyed hearing the Bible. As far as she could tell, neither man did much to practice their faith. She had initiated saying grace before meals and now the Sunday Bible study. *Lord, use these times to pull Elbert and Mr. Ramsey closer to Thee.*

The summer remained busy, and Anna worked hard, both in the garden and the house. She made pickles from their prolific cucumbers, storing them in large crocks in the root cellar cut into a hill. She gathered the onions and hung them in bunches. She pulled carrots and added them to the other cache, knowing she would have to use them quicker than some of the other vegetables or they would lose their crispness. However, even softer ones would taste good in a stew later on. They all dug, picked up, and stored the potatoes.

When the green beans came in, Anna strung those she didn't cook for them to eat. She hung the strings in the sun on the clothesline. When they were dried, she'd take them to the root cellar, too. She'd have to cook them longer than regular beans, but the leather britches would taste good on a cold winter's day.

She made some cherry cobblers and cherry preserves, and the men made cherry cider. The cherry trees seemed to grow wild here. In August, they would do the same with the apples.

The men planted more corn than anything, however. Besides having some rows in the garden to eat, they planted both a large and a small field of it. They could have some ground into feed for the animals, but the bulk of it would be ground into cornmeal.

"A family had tried to farm this land before we come," Elbert explained, "but they give up, so some of the land had been cleared before. And, me and Pa clear a little more each year."

"Do you plant some fall crops?" Anna asked.

"We do, but the growing season ain't very long here, and winter can come early. We still try to get in a crop of cabbage, turnips, and greens, however."

"Oh. You put the cabbage in right after the cucumbers and squash quit bearing."

"Yeah, and the turnips and greens go in where the potatoes were."

Anna looked over the garden. The black, fertile soil promised heavy harvests. "Do you plant collards?"

"No, Pa don't like them as good. We sow turnip and mustard greens. We like to cook them together."

Anna hadn't been feeling well, and it showed. "You gettin' puny, girl?" Mr. Ramsey asked at breakfast one morning. Anna had toasted her a piece of bread instead of eating the sausage, gravy, and biscuits the men were having.

Anna suspected the cause of her nausea, but she wanted to tell Elbert first. "I hope not."

"Well, don't think you can slack offa your duties. If you ain't in the bed runnin' a fever, you need to take care of your work."

"I plan to." She hoped her voice didn't sound as snappy as she felt.

She caught Elbert in the garden without his father. "I think we're goin' to have a baby," she whispered.

"Yes! Man alive! That's wonderful!" He started to pick her up but seemed to decide at the last minute that might not be the best idea.

Mr. Ramsey came running out of the barn. "What's the matter?" He slowed when he saw nothing looked awry. "What's all the yellin' about?"

"Anna's goin' to have a baby." Elbert looked prouder than a newly elected president.

Mr. Ramsey slapped his son on the back. "Way to go, son. I knowed you could do hit."

Anna didn't know how to take that. She started to turn to go back to the house.

"Wait a minute, girl. When's the happy event?"

She turned. "I don't know for sure, but sometime in the winter for sure."

"That's good. We'll have more time fer hit then, and hit'll be less a bother."

"Who will help with the delivery?" she wondered aloud.

Mr. Ramsey scratched his head. "Well, I could likely do hit, 'cause Elbert here don't have the experience I do with the animals' birthin's, and he might not know what to do on his own. I thank I heared tell of a granny woman over on the other side of the mountain that people turn to at birthin's. I guess we could have her come the week you thank hit's due."

"I'd prefer that."

"Figured you would. Don't know whar you got all your highfaluting ways at an orphan house. Too picky if you ask me. And don't thank this means you can skimp on your jobs. Women's been havin' babies since the beginnin' of time."

Anna looked at Elbert, but he looked away. She turned and walked into the cabin.

No one treated Anna special in the days to follow, and she shouldn't have expected them to, but she had expected it from Elbert. He practically glowed with the idea of being a father, but things continued with them as before. He never treated her harshly or bad, but he never showed her love or treasured her in any way. He never told her he loved her. Their lovemaking seemed to satisfy him but left her feeling even more hollow and alone.

She kept telling herself that her situation could be much worse, and she thanked God for finding a place to live that gave her a warm cabin and food at each meal. No one physically abused her, and Elbert never treated her in a harsh or unseemly manner. But she couldn't stop herself from wishing for more.

Maybe Elbert would fall in love with her at some point. People could change; God could change them. Could she fall in love with her husband? Perhaps. She cared for him now, and certainly didn't want anything bad to happen to him. Maybe she loved him, but she knew she wasn't *in* love with him. Had her childhood dreams caused her to be unreasonable? Was she expecting too much?

By September, they had most of the crops in. Only the turnips and greens were left. "We'll likely need to get them in soon," Elbert said. "Hit'll come a hard frost sometime in October and maybe even sooner." Already the days were getting cooler, and the nights felt cold.

All summer and fall, when they had the time, the men cut and stacked wood. Although Anna didn't help with the gathering or cutting, she did most of the carrying and stacking. Surely they wouldn't need this much wood, but Elbert said they would.

Anna now spent most of her spare time picking up walnuts and chestnuts from the forest. She'd shell the walnuts come winter. She even found a couple of persimmon trees and made a persimmon pudding. She found she enjoyed getting out in the woods. It brought her a deeper peace than she'd ever felt in the cabin.

"Don't go usin' all our sugar," Mr. Ramsey said. "Hit's too expensive to use for more'n special occasions." But Anna noticed he enjoyed the desserts she fixed.

"I'm goin' to Boone tomorrow," Mr. Ramsey announced. "I'll pick up enough staples to see us through the winter and well into spring. Will ya'll be needin' anythang else?"

"I could use some cloth to make some things for the baby."

He nodded. "Make me a list of what you want. The store clerk will be able to fill hit."

Anna made the list. Besides white cotton for diapers and shifts, she listed enough fabric to make her two loose skirts and blouses for when she got big. She also added thread, buttons, needles, and some yarn for knitting.

She would like to go and pick out the things herself, but she knew Mr. Ramsey wouldn't like that idea. It would have been nice to travel down the mountain and see the town of Boone.

"What's all this?" Mr. Ramsey seemed even more disgruntled than usual when she handed him the list. "Read hit to me." He shoved it back at her.

"I'll git the cloth for the baby. Hit won't take much for hit, but the clothes you got will do you."

"My dresses I brought with me from the orphan house can't be let out, and I only have three, counting the one I got married in. I'll make the skirt and blouse so they can be taken up after the baby comes."

"Humph. I'll think about hit. What in the world do you need so much yarn fer?"

"For knitting a wrap, cap, and socks for the baby, and I thought you and Elbert could use some socks this winter."

"I hain't made of cash, woman. You're goin' to be the ruin of us."

Elbert shifted from one foot to the other. "Anna's worked hard 'longside a us, and she sets a decent table. She hain't askin' fer that much, Pa. Don't you thank she's earned hit?"

"I thank we're givin' her a home, and she's just earned her keep. That's what I thank."

Elbert didn't reply, and Anna didn't say any more either. Mr. Ramsey would get what he decided to, and nothing they said would make any difference. She would just have to make do the best she could.

"Pa ain't nearly as broke as he lets on," Elbert said the next day after his father left in the wagon. "We don't owe nobody nothing', and Pa's got a little cash put back. I don't know how much."

"You ever think about getting your own place, maybe closer to town?"

He shook his head. "No, I wouldn't do that. Pa needs me, and hit takes the two of us to get the work done."

She didn't point out that Elbert and her made two. She knew he wouldn't take kindly to her pushing him to leave this place.

"Come on." He looked as excited as a little boy at Christmas. "Let's take advantage of Pa being gone and me not being tired." She followed him into the bedroom.

When Mr. Ramsey returned, he had most of the things from her list. He'd bought all the fabric for the baby and over half the yarn. He'd bought her some cloth, although she didn't think it would make two skirts and two blouses. He hadn't got the notions, but he searched in a trunk and came out with a small basket containing needles, threads, and buttons.

"That belonged to my wife. Figured you could use what's there. Elbert and I could probably make some buttons out of wood this winter if'n you need 'em, but they'd be bigger ones."

"Thank you, sir." Truth be told, this was more than she'd expected. She couldn't wait to get started on the baby's things but wondered if she shouldn't make hers first. She'd already begun to show.

Chapter Four: Adversity

Winter came with brutal force. The wind gusted hard and whipped everything, making the evergreens bow to its force. Sometimes fine snow might accompany it. Anna felt for Elbert trudging out every morning to feed, milk, and gather the eggs.

"That's just blow snow," Mr. Ramsey said. "Hit never amounts to much."

Anna liked to watch it anyway. She rarely saw even a flake in Charleston. However, she tried to contain her excitement, for she knew it would irritate her father-in-law.

The hens weren't laying as much in this weather, and Anna quit cooking eggs for breakfast. Porridge tasted mighty good on the cold mornings, however.

She rarely ventured out now. She even washed the clothes and hung them around the fire to dry. Elbert carried in the water for her.

"You coddle that girl too much, Elbert," Mr. Ramsey accused.

"She's my wife, Pa. You'd do the same for Ma."

"Your ma wuz twice the woman she'll ever be." Did the man take pleasure out of belittling Anna? "A purty woman can't be trusted. You mark my word. She'll run off with the first sweet-talking man that comes her way."

Is that what he had against her? Did he think her too pretty? "I would never do such a thing." She had to speak out this time. "I try my best to live by the Bible. I'm Elbert's wife until death do us part."

"Humph. We'll see."

Anna stood at the window looking at the cloudy sky. "Do you think it will snow for Christmas?"

"Hard to tell." Elbert didn't look up from the harness he mended.

"Could we decorate for Christmas?"

"Whata you have in mind?"

"Just bring in some evergreen boughs to place on the ledges and some holly with red berries."

"I hain't got no use for such foolishness. I don't want that mess around me." Mr. Ramsey shook his head as if to emphasize his feelings on the matter.

"But the evergreens will smell so good. It'll smell like Christmas."

"Not to me hit won't. I forbid hit."

She looked at Elbert. He shrugged.

If she could, she would have gathered some herself and at least put them in her and Elbert's bedroom, but she had grown big and unwieldy, so she'd better not attempt that now.

Elbert planned to go bring back the granny woman next month. Anna figured she wouldn't be due until sometime in February, since they'd married in May.

The meager Christmases in the orphan house had been better than this one, but Anna did what she could to make it special. She baked a walnut cake and glazed it. They would eat it for Christmas dinner. She put a candle in all four of the windows in the house and lit them on Christmas Eve until they went to bed. Mr. Ramsey complained, but she'd made the candles, and she lit them anyway. She read the first half of the Christmas story and would read the last part tomorrow, on Christmas Day.

She cooked a big breakfast Christmas morning and had it ready when Elbert came back with the milk and three eggs. After breakfast, she finished reading the Christmas story and handed out her presents. She'd knitted two pair of socks for both Elbert and Mr. Ramsey. She'd also made Elbert a scarf.

"I didn't thank to get you anything." Elbert looked sheepish.

"That's all right. It's better to give than to receive." Anna wanted to feel that way and not be hurt. However, couldn't Elbert have made some kind of effort or small gesture? Even at the orphan house, they'd always gotten something, at least a stick of candy.

"Guess all that cloth and yarn I bought can count as yours." Mr. Ramsey wouldn't even look her in the eye.

Anna spent the rest of the day sewing. She had the baby's layette about half finished, but she wore her one skirt and alternated the two blouses she'd been able to make. A peace settled over her as she sewed. She would soon have the best gift she'd ever received; she'd be a mother.

She knew the baby had life from the way it moved and kicked. Her nausea had long since left her, and, except for being unwieldy, bulky, and awkward, she felt fine. Although she had to admit, she tired much more easily. She tried not to give into anxiety, but she didn't know what to expect. Elbert assured her the granny woman had plenty of experience and would guide her through everything, and she knew God would be with her. In that she had no doubt.

On January the fourteenth, Anna woke up with back pain, but she said nothing and went to cook breakfast. By mid-morning, the pain had moved to her core. When her abdomen began to twitch, she knew something out of the ordinary was taking place.

She had a stew simmering for dinner, so she went ahead and made some cornbread, but when the men came in from the barn, she didn't feel like eating. She excused herself and started for the bedroom.

"You're not goin' just leave the table for us to clean up, are you?" Mr. Ramsey sounded aggravated.

"I'm afraid the baby is coming, and it's too early." Anna knew worry covered her face. "Do you think you could get the granny lady?"

Mr. Ramsey shook his head. "Hit'd take too long, and I thank a blizzard is blowing in."

Elbert looked pale, as if he didn't know what to do.

"Might be just a false alarm," Mr. Ramsey added. "Elbert's ma had some of those."

Elbert's mother had also lost several babies. That thought didn't make Anna feel a bit better.

Lying in bed became uncomfortable, and Anna decided to sit up a while. When she stood, however, her water broke, and she panicked. "Elbert!"

He came running, but took one look at the situation and called his father. "Looks like we're goin' have to deliver this baby anyways," Mr. Ramsey told his son.

Lord, help me! Anna couldn't wrap her mind around the horrors of it all. "I want Elbert to do the delivering."

"I-I-I'm not sure I can." Elbert sounded so helpless she almost felt sorry for him.

"I have no more inclination to see you in this position than you do to have me here." Mr. Ramsey took a step back. "I'll just pull up a chair in that corner over thar, and tell Elbert what to do. That way, neither one of us will be too embarrassed."

Thank you, Lord. Help me not to panic here. Help me to stay focused on Thee and not the situation. I know Thou desireth the best for me, and I choose to trust in Thee. Guide Elbert and Mr. Ramsey to do what needs to be done, and bring us a healthy baby, I pray. Amen.

As the pain intensified, Anna tried to do her part and follow Mr. Ramsey's directions, but she got lost in the pain. She remembered Elbert saying, "I see the head." She knew when the baby slipped out with more pain than she knew possible. She felt Elbert cover her with a sheet and heard him ask his father to come cut the cord. She heard Mr. Ramsey say, "That wuz quicker than most first births." Then she slept.

She woke to a baby crying. She opened her eyes and saw Elbert with his head in his hands, sitting in a chair beside the bed. Then, her eyes fell on the tiny bundle beside her. She started to unwrap its blanket.

"Hit's a girl." Elbert didn't sound either happy or upset.

Mr. Ramsey must have heard some movement, because he came in. "Couldn't even give us a boy, could you? Just a worthless girl. What good will a girl be to us on the farm? Elbert needs a son to help him when I am gone and to carry on the Ramsey name."

"Pa…"

"Well, never mind. Hit's such a puny little thang, probably won't make hit anyways."

Anna wrapped her daughter in her arm, buried her head in her pillow, and cried.

"Don't cry, Anna." Elbert patted her shoulder. "I'm sorry for what Pa said. He don't mean to be so cruel."

She faced her husband. "Why doesn't he like me?"

Elbert ran his hand down his face. "Sometimes I thank he's jealous I found such a pretty wife and jealous I divide my attention between you and him. I don't know. He's not been the same since Ma died." He nodded at the baby. "You probably need to feed her."

She looked down at her daughter, who had quit crying as she cuddled her.

"She's probably wore out, too, but she's so little, she needs to eat." Was that concern she heard in his voice?

Anna swallowed, as she moved to nurse. "Do you think she'll make it?"

Elbert looked at his daughter. "Only God knows that, I guess. If'n you can get her to take enough milk, she should have a chance."

"What do you want to name her?"

"I don't keer. You name her. The only names I'd thought of wuz boy names." He turned and walked out to join his father.

Anna fed the baby, but she didn't take very much at all. Anna waited about thirty minutes, woke her, and then fed her again.

She heard banging in the kitchen, and Elbert poked his head in the door. "Thar's enough stew left for supper. You want me to brang you some?"

She nodded. "Just bring me a cup of the broth and some milk."

"What do you think about calling her Ellie after you?" Anna asked Elbert when he returned with the food.

"That's fine. You can name her what you want."

As the day waned, Anna wondered if enough heat was filtering into the bedroom for Ellie so she got up, took the baby some clothes, and moved to a place near the fireplace.

When she went to put her clothes on, she noticed the men had only done a halfway job of cleaning her up, so she gave Ellie a better bath before putting on another diaper and shift, and then wrapping her in the blanket she'd knitted.

The men came in from milking. Mr. Ramsey carried the milk bucket, and Elbert carried a crude cradle. "Pa remembered my old cradle was stored in the back of the barn loft. I'll just clean hit up for the baby."

"Thank you."

"You feel like strainin' this milk?"

She couldn't believe Mr. Ramsey expected her to. "Not at the present."

"I'll do it, Pa. I don't mind. Anna needs to rest and take care of the baby."

Ellie took tiny amounts of milk here and there, but she slept almost all the time. If she awoke, she cried, and it worried Anna. She'd had some experience with the babies at the orphan home, and this didn't seem normal to her.

Mr. Ramsey complained. He grumbled when the baby cried, at the washed diapers hung around to dry, and about the time Anna had to devote to Ellie. But Anna decided the unhappy man would find fault no matter what, and she tried to pay him no mind.

Elbert puzzled her more. He took no interest in his daughter, as if the child belonged solely to Anna. He treated Anna the same as always, but he usually ignored Ellie. She'd hoped naming Ellie after him would make him proud, but she guessed the Ramsey men couldn't find it in their hearts to be proud of a girl.

By the time Ellie turned a month old, Anna still couldn't tell that she'd gained any weight or improved. However, despite Mr. Ramsey's gloomy forecast, she tenaciously hung on to life, and Anna prayed. Elbert didn't want to talk about it, and she didn't mention the problem to Mr. Ramsey, because he'd have too much to say and all of it negative.

In March, when Anna had hoped for the promise of spring, another blizzard hit. The wind seemed to cut right through the cabin, and none of them could get warm enough. Every time one of the men opened a door to go outside, the cold draft engulfed the inside.

"I've never knowed winter to leave the mountains in March," Elbert told her.

Ellie developed the croup. Each little cough tore at Anna's heart, and Ellie couldn't nurse for coughing. She held her baby and cried in silence, although she knew the tears did no one any good.

She racked her brain trying to think of something that might help. She simmered onions and forced Ellie to breathe the steam, being careful to stay back far enough not to burn or irritate the baby's skin. Ellie hated it, and voiced her opinion which made her cough all the more.

Late one night, Anna sat up with Ellie, trying to rock her in a straight chair. What she wouldn't give for a rocker. With tears streaming down her face again, Anna looked up to find Elbert standing over her. Had she disturbed him and he'd complain like his father?

He put his calloused hand on her shoulder. "I'm praying for her."

A peace washed over Anna. She held Ellie in one arm and put her other hand over Elbert's. Perhaps he cared more than he showed. The tender moment almost brought another kind of tears to her eyes.

Anna only worked during the snippet of times Ellie slept. She managed to do the most necessary things, but she let some things go. Surprisingly, Mr. Ramsey didn't say anything about her neglecting her duties, but she had a feeling many things had been let go when just the two men lived by themselves.

Then, Ellie took a turn for the worse, and Anna didn't think she'd make it through the night. Anna prayed and prayed and tried to remember Bible verses of encouragement, but she didn't know what she would do if they had to bury Ellie. With the thought too horrible to contemplate, she tried to push it away. It wouldn't go.

Every breath sounded labored and produced a loud wheeze, and Anna kept Ellie on her shoulder most of the time. She would pat her on the back when coughs racked her little body. Because she couldn't eat much, Anna gave her a little honey, hoping it might help soothe her cough and give her some strength. She continued having her breathe the onion steam, but Ellie no longer cried like before. She seemed too weak. With the weak willow bark tea she tried to spoon into her, Anna had done everything at her disposal.

By the grace of God, Ellie made it through the night.

"Youngin's often get worser before they git better," Mr. Ramsey announced the next morning.

Anna's mouth may have dropped open. If Mr. Ramsey could give encouragement, maybe God would produce another miracle and heal Ellie. "I pray that you're right."

By dinnertime, Ellie did seem a little improved, or was Anna looking so hard for it she saw it when she shouldn't? That night Anna sat before the fire, holding Ellie with a pillow in her lap in case she fell asleep and her arms sagged. This would be her second night without sleep and she felt beyond exhaustion.

Anna must have dozed off sometime in the morning, because she woke to Ellie's cough, but it sounded better, looser.

"Told you she'd be gittin' better," Mr. Ramsey said at breakfast.

Anna gave him a smile, glad he may have been right. *Thank, Thee, Lord!*

Ellie continued to improve, although much too gradually to suit Anna. Finally, after she fully recovered, Ellie had a spurt of growing, and Anna felt her daughter had turned the corner.

Spring would arrive soon with all its promise. Anna couldn't wait. Ellie's healing had already brought spring to her soul.

Levi trekked through the snow. This one had only left about six or seven inches, and he'd decided to go hunting. He did that as much as possible. If Violet didn't quit trying to flirt and snare him, he might have to consider finding him someplace else to live, but he hated to leave Noah when they'd finally grown closer, and he loved the Appalachians.

Women! First Leanore and now Violet. When had they gotten so bold, so improper and unseemly? He had tried subtly letting Violet know he had no interest in her

– not the kind she wanted anyway. When that didn't work, he'd told her directly.

"I'll make you change your mind." She turned and walked away before he could say anything else.

He'd stayed away from the house as much as the winter weather would allow. Being out in the cold so much seemed to have toughened him, so God brought something good from the bad situation.

Noah had been no help in the matter. His brother thought he should marry Violet and build a cabin on the property. Then, they could farm together.

On his way home, he detoured to the ledge he liked. He hadn't shot anything today, but the peace of being out here in the white beauty hugged him.

He had just turned to head back to the house when he heard a cry from a distance. The sound startled him and he stopped to listen again. The eerie scream had to be a large cat, a mountain lion more than likely. The cry had been too loud and deep to be a bobcat that most people around here called a "wildcat."

He resumed his walk back to the cabin. He needed to be more cautious when out hunting, for that predator had sounded hungry. Winter made many of the wild animals hungry, but at least the bears were hibernating now.

"Violet, you need to quit following me. If you're trying to garner my attention, you're going about it in the wrong way. Your pushing just moves me farther away."

"Why don't you like me?" Tears gathered in her eyes, and Levi felt like a scoundrel.

"It's not that. I like you just fine. I'm just not interested in marrying you."

"We wouldn't have to marry to be together would we?"

Did she mean what he thought she meant? Now he knew he didn't want her for a wife. She had just turned bold into brazen. Had she no shame? "We would as far as I'm concerned. I try to live by God's Word."

She turned so red it couldn't have all been from the cold in the barn. "I...I.... Oh..." She turned and almost ran back to the cabin.

Levi hoped Violet finally understood she needed to quit her flirty ways. At least she appeared embarrassed by her behavior in the barn. Somehow he felt this had just been another way of getting her hooks into him so she could lead him to the altar. Still, he wanted no part in it.

For almost a week, Violet didn't bother Levi again, but it didn't take long for her to resume eying him with interest. She wore dresses a little too tight to reveal her well-proportioned figure, and she batted her eyelashes so often it looked like gnats had flown into her eyes. He kept praying things would get better.

Finally spring came, and the work intensified. Levi and Noah spent most of the daylight hours in the small fields. Sometimes, Daisy and Violet would come out to help with the planting, but the work kept them all too busy to be concerned with much else.

The hens set and hatched biddies, the second cow had a calf, and the sow had a litter. Spring always bustled after the lull of winter, and Levi appreciated the activity.

Chapter Five: Death on the Mountain

"Why don't you spend any time with Ellie?" Anna finally asked Elbert the question that lay heavily on her mind. She didn't know why she felt so nervous. Elbert didn't act the way his father did, and she didn't think he'd lash out at her.

"Me and Pa were hoping for a boy, and I guess I don't know what to do with a girl. I'm hopin' we'll have a boy soon. I like the tryin' to get one." He gave her a boyish grin.

She could hear the amusement in his voice on that last part. It was the closest thing to being romantic she could remember, but it could also be taken in a completely different way. She wished she could say the same about their intimate moments, but she couldn't. If she thought he truly loved her, it would make a big difference.

"Me and Elbert's goin' to take some thangs into Boone and git some coffee, sugar, and a few thangs fer the farm," Mr. Ramsey announced one morning. "We'll try to git back before night, but hit might be tomorrow before you see us."

"All right. I'll pack you some food." She didn't dare tell them she'd like some things, too. What she needed could wait or she'd figure out a way to improvise. She'd gotten good at doing that.

With a fair sky and warm sunshine, Anna decided to work outside most of the day. The garden looked good, but it could use hoeing, and she needed to pick some of the early vegetables, like garden peas.

Ellie loved to get outside and would sit on a quilt and play. Anna enjoyed hearing her babble with sounds only Ellie could understand. Maybe she'd be walking by Christmas.

Despite her conversation with Elbert, both men still largely ignored the little girl, and Ellie had learned to turn to Anna. It broke Anna's heart that Elbert didn't show his daughter more attention. How would this affect her as she grew up?

The men didn't return that day, but Anna expected to see them by dinnertime on the following day, since they'd likely get an early start. However, it was early afternoon before she heard the wagon roll in.

She looked out to see Mr. Ramsey, but she didn't see Elbert beside him. Had Elbert already gotten down? She scooped up Ellie and went outside. The moment she got closer, she knew something had to be wrong. Mr.

Ramsey's face looked ashen, and he seemed near tears. She had never seen him this emotional and would have never imagined him like this. He didn't say a word as she approached the wagon. That's when she saw Elbert lying in the back, ripped to pieces, especially his torso.

She put her hand to her mouth to keep from screaming at the top of her voice. She couldn't even find the words to ask what had happened.

"Mountain lion." Mr. Ramsey answered without the question being asked. "Came out of nowhere and attacked when we wuz stopped fer a break. I got off a shot as soon as I could, but hit wuz too late. Didn't kill the beast, just skeered hit away, but I will. As soon as I bury my son." His voice cracked.

Anna swallowed, but it did little to stop the flow of tears. "Bring him inside, and I'll clean him up."

The man clenched his jaw but nodded. "I'll build a coffin and start digging the grave."

All the time Anna washed the body, the tears flowed. She grieved for what could have been and for a life snuffed out much too early. She cared for Elbert, and he had fathered her daughter. It hurt to see this happen.

She dressed him in his best clothes, wishing he had a suit or something dressier than his practical work clothes. When she finished, he looked like himself, except for his pale color and a few gashes. The clothes covered most of them.

Ellie sat on the floor and played with some wooden stirring spoons, sometimes babbling to herself, but every now and then she'd stop and watch Anna for a while. She would now grow up without her papa, and a standoffish father would have been better than no father at all. Wouldn't it?

Anna couldn't imagine how this would change things for her and Ellie. What would living alone with her father-in-law be like? He'd never seemed to like either one of them very much, so would he ask them to leave, and where would they go if he did? Surely he would want them to stay for Anna's housekeeping abilities if nothing else. He did seem to appreciate her cooking most of the time now.

She shook herself. She shouldn't be worrying too far ahead right now. She needed to deal with Elbert's death first. She'd just try to take care of things as they came and do the best she could. God would provide a way.

They buried Elbert the next day. She read some Bible verses and said a prayer. Her voice cracked at times, and the tears wet her face, but she made it through the brief service.

"I do believe Elbert accepted Christ as his Savior," she told Mr. Ramsey.

He gave a curt nod, but she couldn't tell if the words gave him comfort or not. He hadn't said much since he'd brought Elbert's body home.

"Fix me as much food as you thank will keep for a while." Mr. Ramsey told her at supper. "I'm goin' after that mountain lion tomorrow, and I'm not comin' home until I find hit."

"Very well, but do be careful. I don't know what Ellie and I would do if something happened to you, too."

"If'n I don't come back, this place is yourn."

"Thank you." She didn't know what else to say or if she could keep the place going by herself or not. Maybe she could provide enough for her and Ellie to eat, but she appreciated her father-in-law telling her this.

"You wuz Elbert's pick, and I'll honor that."

After Mr. Ramsey left the next morning, the cabin felt as empty as a fasting man's stomach. After completing her morning chores, Anna sat down, held Ellie close, and thanked God for her daughter.

When Ellie became squirmy, Anna took her for a walk outside the cabin. They ended up standing before Elbert's grave. "Oh, Elbert, why did this have to happen? Even though you didn't treat me special and didn't show Ellie much attention at all, I miss you. What are we going to do without you? If nothing else, you provided for us the best you could. But rest in peace. Your earthly struggles are over." Hers had just gotten a whole lot worse.

Anna and Ellie fell into a peaceful routine. With just the two of them, it didn't take as much work to cook or clean. However, when Mr. Ramsey didn't come back in two weeks, Anna began to worry. What would she do if he didn't return? Could she stay here in the isolated cabin by herself? Could she keep enough food for them? Would she even be able to find her way to town for needed supplies, and, if she did, how would she pay for them?

She looked around. She still had Elbert's rifle, and he'd taught her the basics of firing it. She wouldn't be skilled enough to go out hunting, and she couldn't with Ellie anyway, but sometimes a deer would come close to the cabin, especially when the garden had produce. Perhaps she could also use it to protect Ellie and her.

She harvested the garden by herself. They hadn't planted the larger field this year before the accident, but the regular garden had done well. The small field would provide feed for some of the animals, as well as cornmeal for her and Ellie, but she didn't know where to take the corn to be ground. Elbert had said they took it to a neighbor who had a small gristmill, but she hadn't seen a neighbor the whole time she'd been here.

Summer came to an end, and Anna went through Elbert's things. He'd been a taller man than his father. Should she save his clothes to hem up for Mr. Ramsey, or should she use them for something else?

She decided to use two of his shirts to make shifts for Ellie. Once she started growing, Ellie grew quickly, and she'd need some warm ones for winter. Anna packed up the other clothes to use later. If Mr. Ramsey didn't want the pants, it would be easy to find a use for them. She wished she had a spinning wheel and loom to make some cloth, but she had no idea of how to get them or the wool or flax.

At the bottom of Elbert's small trunk, she found some money. He must have been saving it for a long time from where they'd sold an animal or crops. It didn't amount to much, because they mainly bartered for what they needed, but it would help.

The days slid away, and weeks turned into three months. Anna began to suspect something had happened to Mr. Ramsey. Otherwise, surely he'd have returned by now to get more supplies and go back out again if nothing else.

Perhaps she should pack a few things, take Ellie and go to Boone before the weather became too cold. But where would they stay, and how would she pay for it?

She didn't even know if she had enough firewood to last a winter. Elbert and Mr. Ramsey had always taken care of that.

Yet, neither did she know what she would do if she left. If she couldn't find a job somewhere, and that would be hard for a woman with a child, she and Ellie might be worse off by leaving. So much to consider.

She prayed but didn't get a clear answer. She decided to just stay put until she felt God wanted her to go. She'd try weathering one winter here, and then make her final decision in the spring before time to plant the bulk of the garden. In the meantime, maybe Mr. Ramsey would show up.

Anna had dinner almost ready when she heard a firm knocking at the front door. Who would be visiting? No one had ever come in the time she'd been here, and Mr. Ramsey wouldn't just knock. She grabbed Elbert's gun and tucked it under her arm before she answered the door. She kept it loaded.

Two scruffy men stood there. They snatched their hats off their heads and smiled as if they liked what they saw. She tightened her grip on the rifle.

"Howdy ma'am," the oldest looking one said. "We're yer neighbors. I'm Orin Hicks, and this here's my younger brother, Clem."

She raised her eyebrow to question why they were here but said nothing. Her blood pumped so hard she didn't know if she could speak or not.

"Ain't you goin' to invite us in?" Orin tried to look around her into the cabin.

"Somethin' smells mighty good," Clem added.

These two men didn't. Anna wondered when they'd last had a bath. They appeared much dirtier and even more disheveled than Mr. Ramsey.

"We met Hiram out huntin', and he said a mountain lion mauled his son and left a widder and child at home." Clem tried to look into the cabin. "We come to see if'n he made hit back. Figured you might need a man to see you through the winner if he didn't. You can have your pick of us."

"But I'm the oldest and should marry first by rights." Orin gave his brother a stabbing look before he turned back to Anna. "We can even go to Boone or Mountain City, and I'll marry you proper."

Anna cleared her throat. "I'm not interested in another husband with Elbert fresh in the grave. Besides, I'm expecting Mr. Ramsey back any day now."

Orin shook his head. "Ma'am, if he ain't back my now, hit's likely he ain't comin' back. And, with winner coming on soon, you don't want to be alone to fend fer yourself. Why, I bet you don't even have enough farwood cut. Thank of your little girl now."

"I meant what I said, Mr. Hicks. Now if you will kindly go on your way, I need to tend my daughter."

Their faces grew hard, and they both took a step toward her. She raised the rifle enough to point it at them. At this close range, she'd be bound to hit one of them.

"You'll regret this," Orin spit out.

"Not very neighborly of you not to invite us in," Clem added. They both stared at her before they turned and left.

She scurried inside, shut the door, dropped the latch to lock it, and then leaned against it to gain enough strength to move. She'd need to start carrying the gun with her when she went to the barn. Why in the world had Mr. Ramsey told anyone about her being here alone? Perhaps he'd encouraged the Hicks brothers to take her off his hands. She wouldn't put it past the man.

Levi couldn't believe summer had come and gone, fall had arrived, and winter wouldn't be long off. Violet still hadn't left to go home, and it looked as if she planned to make her home here. Daisy had started talking about what a good looking couple he and Violet made, that both of them needed to be thinking about a family if they wanted one, and how wonderful it would be if the brothers and sisters were united.

Noah also hinted at some of the same things, but he tended to be more subtle. Levi tried to consider it but couldn't imagine being tied to someone like Violet. She just didn't appeal to him. The two of them marrying might make sense on the surface, but he didn't think it would work well for either of them in the long run.

He just needed to be patient. At the best time, the Lord would send the right woman into his life, and he didn't like the feeling that all three of them were ganging up on him.

The last day of October felt cold, but Levi decided to go hunting. The family could use the extra meat, and he needed to get away from the cabin. Although Violet tried not to show that she followed him, she'd developed a habit of turning up where he worked on the pretense of taking care of some task.

A few clouds started accumulating as he started out, but no wind blew, and the sun peeped through often enough to warm him some. The farther he went, however, the more the wind picked up, until a slight breeze became heavy gusts. He looked up, and gray clouds appeared thick, hung heavy, and blocked out all the sun. He'd better head back. It looked like a storm might be moving in.

He turned around and had gone a few hundred feet when the first snowflakes started falling. The tiny pellets felt like they had some ice in them too, because they stung his face with the force of the wind.

In a hurry to get back, he picked up his speed, but his foot caught on a protruding tree root. He fell, rolling down a hill, and felt his head hit something hard.

Levi awoke but lay there trying to remember what had happened. He felt numb with cold, and snow had accumulated around him. When he sat up, his head ached, and he felt dizzy. He touched the back of his head to find a large knot. Looking around, he saw the rock he must have hit his head on when he fell and wondered how long he'd been unconscious. No way of telling.

He managed to get to his feet and take a few tentative steps. Once he got his balance, he started off slowly, but the storm had turned into a blizzard, and he couldn't see well enough to tell where he needed to go. Yet, he needed to keep moving. He'd freeze otherwise.

He must not have been unconscious for too long or else he might have never awakened, for the freezing snow would have covered him. The fine flakes turned into big heavy flakes as he walked, and he could barely tell where to put his feet in the blizzard. He kept walking, however, because doing so kept him warmer.

With no idea of what time it might be or how far he'd walked, Levi decided to build a lean-to for shelter. When night came, the darkness would fall fast. Perhaps the snow accumulating on the shelter would even provide insulation. If he built it at the correct angle, it would keep most of the wind and snow off him, and he didn't think the temperature dipped too far below freezing, although the wind made it feel like it.

Pulling out his hatchet, he took a whack at a sapling to use as a pole. The blade didn't penetrate as he expected, but bounced off and came to rest in his leg. Pain shot up him, and he fell to the ground. Bright red blood quickly spread over the white snow.

He tied the top of the gash with his large handkerchief and then wrapped his scarf around the wound as tightly as he could to form a makeshift bandage. Building a shelter wouldn't work now. He'd bleed to death. He picked up a downed branch and trimmed it to make a crude crutch. He didn't lean on it too heavily now, but he knew he'd grow weaker from the loss of blood, and his wounded leg might give out soon. Hopefully the cold would help slow the bleeding.

He heard the cry of that mountain lion again, but the animal sounded far off. However, it or some other predator still might pick up his trail of blood. Every turn of events seemed to make his already dire situation more precarious.

Lord, I desperately need Thy help. I put myself and this dangerous situation in Thy hands. Help me get home, I beseech Thee. I don't know how close I am, but I pray I'm close enough to make it. Please guide me and direct my path. In Jesus' name. Amen.

Levi forced himself to keep moving, when he wanted to collapse. He knew if he lay down he'd die in the snow, but he didn't know how much longer he could keep going. He felt the life draining out of him with every feeble limp.

Chapter Six: Guided

As the early blizzard raged outside, Anna and Ellie stayed in the house. Anna went out to milk when Ellie took her naps, because she didn't want to take her out in this weather.

They'd finished supper, and Anna had put Ellie to bed when she heard a loud thud against the front door. At first she feared opening the door in the dark, afraid it might be a dangerous, wild animal or the Hicks brothers, although she doubted they'd come out in a snowstorm. When she heard nothing else, she set her gun within easy reach beside the door and eased it open to a crack to peer out.

The man lying face down on the porch scared her so much, she slammed the door closed. She started to bar the door but she had second thoughts. How could she turn her back on someone in need? If she did, she'd be no better than the priest and the Levite who passed the wounded man by in the Bible story of the Good

Samaritan. She needed to do what she could to help the man and trust God that she'd be safe.

She dragged him into the house by grasping him under his arms, but she found it hard. He appeared to be a bigger man than Elbert. She left him in the floor while she secured the door. One look showed his blood soaked leg. She gasped when she unwound the bloody knit scarf and saw the gaping slit. This would need to be stitched up. Could she do it?

She pulled him closer to the fireplace, knowing that she'd not be able to lift him into a bed by herself. She looked at his cut again, and saw that it still bled but slowly now.

She got a basin, filled it with lukewarm water, gathered the soap and a cloth, cut his pants leg so she could get to the wound better, and cleaned off the dried blood around it. Cold water would have been better for the bleeding, but she could tell how cold he'd become, and he needed to warm up. Next, she got her needle and thread and squeezed her eyes shut to say a quick prayer before she began.

Getting started with the first thrust of the needle proved to be hard, but once she got going, it went quickly. When she finished, she rewashed it, cleaned around the rest of his leg where the blood had run and dried, and bandaged it with strips of old sheeting.

She added hot water to the basin, pulled off his boots and socks, and washed his feet, which felt cold but didn't look frostbitten as far as she could tell. She put a pillow under his head and wrapped him in covers.

Stoking the fire and adding some wood, she wondered about going to bed, but she didn't think she could sleep with a strange man in the house. No, better to sit near, where his movement would wake her even if she did go to sleep.

She sat down and looked at him closer. He must be about three inches taller than Elbert and perhaps not quite as thin. He had dark hair and beard, almost black but not quite. Both were trimmed neater than Elbert kept his. His face looked more handsome, too. She pulled her eyes away. She shouldn't be comparing him to Elbert or appraising the man this way.

She checked on Ellie, got herself a quilt, and got as comfortable as she could in a straight chair. For the hundredth time, she wished she had a rocking chair.

Levi awoke on a hard surface with his leg aching. Did he remember his head aching, too? If so, it felt much better than his leg.

He opened his eyes to daylight. By the grace of God, he'd made it through the night and through the blizzard. He looked around and saw a strange room. He lay on the floor near a fireplace, but then his gaze fell on a woman sleeping in a precarious position in a chair with her head hanging toward her lap. Her hair was the prettiest shade of yellow he'd ever seen.

Afraid that she might fall from her chair, he started to rise but fell back, too dizzy to continue. His head still felt sore, too.

She stirred, lifted her head, and looked straight at him. Her blue-gray eyes were startlingly bright, and they widened at the sight of him awake.

"You look like an angel." The words came out without thinking. "I'm guessing you're the guardian angel who saved my life. Thank you." He hoped that would help, because he wanted to wipe away that fear he saw in her eyes.

"Y-yes. You fell onto my porch last night. Who are you?"

"I'm Levi West, ma'am, and where am I?"

"This is the Ramsey place. I don't know too much more than that. I've only been here for a couple of years, ever since I married my husband."

Wouldn't you know it? The first woman that piqued his interest around here would be married. At first glance, he'd wondered if she might have been the one, but he needed to remember what a problem women could be.

He refocused on her, knowing he needed to answer her question instead of letting his thoughts run free. "I live with my brother and his wife up the mountain from the community of Sugar Grove, but I became disoriented in the storm, and I'm not sure where I am now or where my brother's cabin is in relation to here."

She started to get up, but he wanted her to stay and talk some more. "What's your name?"

"Anna. Anna Ramsey."

"Where did you live, Mrs. Ramsey? Before you came here."

"In the orphan house in Charleston." She looked uncomfortable and stood. "I'd better start breakfast."

Just as well. He needed to curtail his curiosity and not try to get to know her better, since the woman was married. However, he lay close enough to the fireplace that he could watch her every move, although she had placed him far enough away last night that she didn't have to walk around him.

He heard a child fussing. Anna stopped what she'd been doing and went to a bed on the other side of the room. She picked up a little girl he hadn't noticed.

"Good morning, Ellie," Anna mumbled into the child's hair as she held her close. "Let's get your diaper changed, and Mama will fix you some porridge. How does that sound?"

Ellie popped her thumb into her mouth and snuggled closer to her mother. When Anna took care of the child's needs and sat her on a quilt near the fireplace but out of Levi's reach, the little girl crawled to him.

"Good morning, Ellie," he told her as she moved to a sitting position close to his chest. She smiled.

"Ellie, don't bother Mr. West."

"She's no bother. She's adorable." In fact, she looked much like a miniature version of her mother. "Let me entertain her while you cook."

Anna hesitated, so he added, "I can't do much to help you, but I can do this."

She nodded and went back to cooking, but she kept glancing their way.

Levi tried to think of what Iris enjoyed, but with three other adults doting on her, he didn't get to play with his niece that often. He started with pat-a-cake. Ellie loved it, and her little giggles made him smile, too.

Before Ellie got tired of pat-a-cake, Anna came with a bowl of porridge. She pulled Ellie back with one hand and set the porridge in her place where Levi could reach it if he turned on his side.

"How do you like your coffee?" She picked Ellie up.

"With just a touch of cream." He thanked God for the food before she returned.

She brought him some coffee. He managed to lie on his side with his left elbow on the floor and his head resting on that hand. That gave him some support, but he still found it hard to eat. While Anna fed Ellie; he tried, but after a few minutes, he had to return to his back, too weak to continue.

"Here." Anna sat beside him and picked up the bowl. "Let me help. I know you must be weak from losing so much blood, and you need to eat to get your strength back."

"Where's your husband?"

"A mountain lion mauled him, and we buried him a few months back. My father-in-law went to hunt the beast. I'm expecting him back any day now." The anguish on her face made him regret he'd asked the question.

A widow, though. That news made him hurt for her, but at the same time he wondered if God had brought him here for a reason. If so, he wished he could help her around the place instead of being laid up.

He took another bite she offered and hated being so incapacitated. It made him feel less of a man, but he tried to eat what she spooned into his mouth. When he'd finished with all he could eat, she helped him raise his head, and he drank about half of his coffee. He might have drunk more if her touch hadn't done strange things to him. But the simple tasks took all his energy. The last thing he remembered before sleep overtook him was Ellie laying her head on his shoulder and nestling into his chest.

Anna stood for a moment and watched Ellie sleeping beside Levi. Ellie had been restless last night without Anna beside her. They'd slept together since Elbert died, but she still couldn't believe Ellie had taken to Levi so quickly. The poor child must crave a father's attention.

Tears gathered in her eyes, and she tried to brush them away. Levi had shown Ellie more direct attention in those brief minutes this morning than Elbert had since she'd been born.

She looked at the man again, wondering if she could trust him. By all indications, she could, but she still needed to be careful. He could be presenting a good image until he got his strength back and his leg healed enough that he could get around.

She closed her eyes and prayed. She prayed for Levi's healing, so he could leave soon; and she prayed for protection, guidance, and direction. With each passing day, she knew Mr. Ramsey would be less likely to return, especially with the harsh winter weather. Something must have happened to him. Whatever would she do?

When she had dinner almost ready, Anna went to wake Levi and Ellie. She found Ellie awake, still resting beside Levi and playing quietly with her hands. Anna smiled when she realized her daughter was trying to play pat-a-cake by herself.

Ellie sat up when she saw Anna, and her movement woke Levi. "I'm sorry I fell asleep like that."

"Don't apologize. You need to eat and sleep to heal. Dinner is almost ready. I came to see if you think you can move to the bed where you'll be more comfortable. You were too heavy last night for me to put you there."

He sat up, but she could tell it took him great effort. "Did you find the tree limb fashioned as a crutch?"

"No, but I didn't look around. I'll go out front and see if it's there. The snow has stopped, but it's still cold."

He raised an eyebrow. "You've been outside to check?"

"I went to the barn to milk, gathered the few eggs, and brought in some firewood."

He looked down. "I sure wish I were able to help with the chores."

"Don't you worry about that. I'm used to doing them now." She turned and walked out to the porch without giving him a chance to answer.

She didn't find the crutch on the porch, but she saw it lying on top of the snow in front of the step. She grabbed it and hurried inside, away from the biting cold.

Even with the crutch, Levi couldn't move well enough to make it to the bed. She didn't know if his leg or his head caused the problem, maybe both, but she got on his other side. "Lean on me." She could tell he hesitated to put much weight on her. "I moved you last night, and with you helping, you don't seem nearly as heavy."

He looked up and saw where they were headed. "I don't want to take your bed. I'll be fine on the floor. You can make me a pallet there."

"Nonsense. This will make it more comfortable for you and easier for me to care for you. There's another bedroom, and Ellie and I will sleep in there. It's where we slept before the attack on Elbert. This is really Mr. Ramsey's bed."

She didn't add that the bedroom had no separate heat. At least Elbert had put a latch on the door, and she'd feel a bit more secure there. She would leave the door open during the day and hope enough heat would make its way into the back room. If she pulled Ellie close under heavy covers, they should be fine.

Sweat broke out on Levi by the time they made it to the bed. Maybe she should have left him on the floor a while longer. He fell back onto the bed, and she lifted his legs up. His wounded leg felt warmer than the other when she took hold of it. "I need to change your bandage."

"Please wait a little while." Levi didn't even open his eyes. "I'm plumb tuckered out."

"What about dinner?"

"Later." He drifted off.

Anna hoped he slept and hadn't fallen unconscious. She picked up Ellie and took her to the kitchen. She'd cooked a rabbit stew, and there'd be enough for supper, too. She had learned to trap them to supplement the meat supply left in the smokehouse.

Anna felt Levi's forehead several times through the afternoon, and it felt cool enough. The act felt intimate, and she fought the urge to run her fingers through his hair to wipe it back away from his face. It pleasured her to look on the handsome man now, but she suspected he would be breathtaking without the beard.

He didn't wake up until after she'd put Ellie to bed. She'd left the door open and the back room had stayed fairly warm.

"Are you hungry?" she asked when she saw his deep blue eyes on her.

"Maybe a little."

She helped him sit up and put pillows at his back before she handed him the stew in a tin cup. He closed his eyes for a minute, but she couldn't tell if he prayed or just needed to rest.

He drank the broth and ate the last of the meat and vegetables with a spoon. He also managed a whole cup of milk but didn't eat much of his cornbread.

"Thank you. You're a good cook. I wish I could do your food justice, but my appetite has waned."

Anna almost jerked from surprise at the compliment. "Uh-h, thank you. Now let me see to your leg."

His leg felt warm to her touch – much too warm. She went to unwrap the bandage and found it stuck from dried blood, so she got a basin of warm water and soaked it enough to remove it.

The wound looked red, and it had started to swell. She sucked in her breath. Infection. A doctor would likely remove his leg from the knee down to prevent further spread of the infection or gangrene, but she didn't have the skill to do that. She didn't know if she even could, although perhaps she'd be able to if it meant saving his life.

"What's wrong?"

How much should she tell him? Would telling the truth make Levi fight harder or give up? She didn't know him well enough to determine that. However, she believed honesty to always be best, but she could temper it a bit. "Your wound appears to be getting a bit red and it feels warm. I don't want infection to set in."

He raised himself on his elbow enough to peek at his leg. Lines crinkled his forehead, and he fell back onto his pillow. "Looks like it already has."

"I learned some healing and medicine at the orphan house as we took care of the younger children, but my knowledge is limited. I'm not sure of what to do."

He reached over and took her hand but didn't look her in the eye. "Whatever happens, don't blame yourself. At least you've given me a fighting chance, and I'm grateful."

His touch felt so gentle, so comforting that it almost brought tears to her eyes. Here he lay in a dire situation, and he tried to comfort her. She reluctantly pulled her hand away.

She needed to keep this man at a distance, since she might be as starved for attention as Ellie, and she didn't know much about Levi. Just because he seemed so perfect didn't mean he was. She didn't even want to be thinking about another man now.

He gasped when she pressed near the slit in his leg, although she tried to be gentle. No pus came, and she could detect no foul odor when she put her nose close to smell. She hoped those were good signs and the infection hadn't started too deep in the wound to notice.

She pondered on what she might use to help him as she washed the last remnants of dried blood from his leg. "The bleeding appears to have stopped, so I'm going to put a thinner bandage back on for now. I'm also going to try a poultice tomorrow. Even it doesn't help, it won't hurt."

She saw the worry in his eyes, so she added, "And we both can pray."

With those words, his look of worry vanished. "You're a Christian then?"

"I am. Are you?"

He nodded. "Since childhood."

"That's good. God will see us through this."

His eyes softened. Maybe she shouldn't have said "us." He looked as if he wanted to take her hand again, so she moved them behind her. She had begun to distrust herself because of her reaction to him, and she needed to hurry and get him settled so she could take herself into the bedroom. She didn't like the thoughts he invoked.

"Just remember that if God chooses to take me home, I'll be in a much better place."

Somehow that thought didn't comfort her much.

"Well, I'll be praying that He wants to leave you here for much longer."

His dark blue eyes smiled, although it never made it to his lips, and then they closed.

Anna slept fitfully that night as she worried about Levi's infection. She spent a long time praying, and that brought some peace, but she lay awake thinking about what ingredients she might have that she could make into a poultice.

She wished she had some comfrey, but she didn't. It could be used to reduce the swelling and heal a wound. Nothing would be growing this winter, either, and she would have to wait to gather any herbs until spring or summer. Plantain could be used in a pinch to draw a wound, too, but she didn't think she'd find any of it growing now either. After that blizzard and the snow it left behind, she couldn't find it if it were. So what did she have?

She'd stored cabbage, turnips, potatoes, and onions in the root cellar, and they might be used to draw out infection. Maybe she'd add some oatmeal. Although she didn't have much, the poultice wouldn't take but a pinch. She could mince the vegetables, add the oatmeal, and moisten it all with honey, which would also be good.

Finally, after praying one more time, she drifted to sleep.

Chapter Seven: Infected

When Anna went out to milk the next morning, she went by the root cellar and put the items she needed in a basket. She strained the milk and then made the poultice even before she started breakfast. With all these ingredients, it would be good to let the paste set for a while.

She started some cornmeal mush, not her favorite, but it would be all right with enough butter and milk added. When she went to feel of Levi's forehead, he awoke.

He started to take her hand, but she moved quickly to pull it away. "Will I live?"

How could he joke about such a serious situation? "I sure hope so."

"Do you now? That's good to hear."

His teasing bordered on flirting, and for some reason, that angered her. "I'm a Christian, Mr. West, and I will do my Christian duty."

He looked contrite. "I'm sorry. I didn't mean to imply anything differently. I appreciate all you're doing on my behalf. I'm just sorry I'm adding more work for you."

"I don't have nearly as much to do without the two men around." Oh my. That sounded worse than what he'd said, and she didn't mean it the way it sounded. "But I would take the extra work to have Elbert back."

He looked away. "I'm sure you would." Did his voice sound disappointed or regretful? Perhaps he just sympathized with her loss.

"Let me get this poultice on, and then we can eat breakfast." If the mush hadn't stuck to the bottom of the pot too much. She gave it a stir when she gathered the things she needed to apply the poultice.

She applied the poultice and bandaged his leg as gently as she could. He didn't complain even though his leg looked redder than yesterday. "I'm going to make you some willow bark tea." She did have some of that. "Your head felt a little warm this morning, and the willow bark will help with a fever and with the swelling."

She must have given him a sharp look, because he looked sheepish. "I'm sorry I tried to tease you. I guess I liked your touch too much."

She certainly didn't know what to say to that. He had a way of getting beyond her reserves. He could get under her skin all too easily, and she just hoped he didn't make his way to her heart. Thankfully, Ellie started to fuss as she finished the bandage, and she had a reason to leave abruptly.

She changed Ellie and put her beside Levi while she helped prop him up in bed so he could eat. She brought his breakfast and took Ellie to feed her, but her daughter tried to lean out of her arms to get back to Levi.

"Bring her back when she's finished, and I'll play with her while you eat yours."

Anna nodded, trying to decide if she liked the way Ellie had taken to him or not. It did make life easier for now, but what would Ellie do when the man left?

By the time Ellie had eaten, Levi had cleaned out his bowl, drank most of his milk, and sipped on his coffee. She took Ellie to the bed and watched her daughter laugh as he played with her. She smiled at Ellie's attempt to talk to him in her unknown baby language.

Anna noticed how tired Levi looked as she finished her mush, so she took the pillows out from behind him, helped him lie down, and took Ellie. The little girl fussed, but she got her busy playing with some wooden spools Anna had strung together for her while she did some laundry. She had to wash often to keep Ellie clean diapers.

Levi looked flushed, so she steeped some willow bark tea. She woke him up before lunch and gave him some, but he went right back to sleep. She'd wait to change the poultice until after lunch then.

Levi didn't eat as much for lunch, and he acted weaker. When she changed the bandage, the leg looked more swollen and inflamed. She didn't have to feel his forehead to know he had a fever. Fear tried to grip her. This didn't look good at all, so she prayed for him.

He didn't wake up for supper, so she let him sleep. He had eaten well the other two meals, so the rest might do him more good. She changed his bandage before she went to bed, and he still didn't wake up.

She could smell and see the pus in his wound now. She tried to tell herself that, in pulling it to the surface, the poultice had begun to work, but she felt sick from seeing it. Fear of what would likely happen gripped her. She didn't want to watch Levi die.

She made the willow bark tea stronger and spooned it into him. At least he swallowed it, one spoonful at a time. She tucked his covers around him, stoked the fire, and went to bed. She could pray there as well as anywhere.

Anna awoke sometime in the night. The air felt so cold it stung her nose and throat when she breathed. She eased out of bed to rekindle the fire, and she'd leave the door open, too. In his condition, Levi wouldn't be able to get out of bed if he tried.

Once she had the fire blazing, she could see Levi better, and she went to check on him. He shivered violently from a fever, and his skin felt so hot to her touch that it almost burned her.

Oh Lord, please help!

She got a basin of cold water and bathed his face. She held his head and managed to get some willow bark tea into him without bothering to heat it. Although he drank some of the liquid, he didn't open his eyes or appear to be conscious.

She worked with him for about an hour, washing his face and feeding him more tea. When the chills stopped and he broke out in a sweat, she hoped that meant his fever had also broken.

She pulled the covers back, just leaving the sheet over him. After washing his face again, she unbuttoned his shirt, and washed the sweat from his chest. He sighed, as if that had made him more comfortable, but she swallowed at the strange feelings it evoked as she felt his muscular chest and shoulders beneath the cloth in her hand. It made her much less comfortable.

Disgusted with herself, she stomped away. The fire could use more wood anyway.

When she felt calmer, she pulled a chair close to Levi's bed and watched him. He seemed to be doing better, and she pulled the covers back over him. She probably needed to change his poultice, but she felt exhausted, and she didn't want to disturb him now that he rested more comfortably. It would likely be daylight soon, so she'd just sit here and make sure Levi didn't get that bad again.

Levi awoke to the gray tones of the first lightening of the day. He had an excruciating headache and felt as weak as coffee made through old grounds.

He felt a presence beside him, and looked over to find Anna's head resting on the bed, although she sat in a chair pulled close. Had he taken a turn for the worse? Why else would she resume a vigil?

He moved his hand toward her hair, being careful not to make a sound. The light, golden tresses were as soft and fine as he'd imagined. He wanted to run his fingers through the mass of it, but he knew better than to try. What about Anna drew him with such force?

After his latest experiences with women, he had almost come to the conclusion that it might be better if he remained single. First Leanore had flung herself at him and created a huge rift between him and his best friend. Then, Violet persisted in flirting, letting him know she wanted to marry him, and almost doing the same thing, except she hadn't promised herself to another. He didn't know if he could ever trust such forward women, and neither of those interested him.

But Anna did interest him, and she certainly didn't flirt or throw herself at him. In fact, she held back too much and seemed too reserved. He recognized the irony. When he finally meets a woman that he'd like to get to know better, she gives no indication that she feels the same way about him.

"Don't be so uncaring and selfish," he told himself. "She's still grieving for her husband who's only been dead a few months."

He rubbed a strand of her hair through his fingers and thumb. Just being close to her brought on a wealth of emotions he had yet to sort out. He wanted to protect her, to ensure her happiness. Her eyes often held a sadness that he wanted to obliterate, but he saw a resolve there, too. Growing up in the orphan house and then coming to a rustic mountain farm couldn't have made for an easy life.

He wanted to pull her close, comfort her, and tell her everything would be all right. He wanted to make everything all right. The urge to pull her in bed with him hit him so strongly he looked away and closed his eyes.

He felt her move and decided to remain as still as a corpse, pretending sleep. His instincts told him she'd be embarrassed otherwise. He both appreciated and disliked how demure and modest she seemed. He could have taken a bit of flirting from Anna.

Anna started breakfast before she came back to the bed to check on him. "Oh, you're awake. How do you feel?"

"I've felt better. How did you fare the night?" Maybe she would tell him why she'd been sleeping in the chair beside his bed.

"I got up to stoke the fire, and you had a high fever. I worked to bring it down, but you remained asleep or unconscious. Nothing seemed to rouse you."

"Thank you." How inadequate those words felt in expressing his feelings.

The worry lines on her face relaxed. "I'm just glad to see you awake and better. I gave you enough willow bark tea to either cure you or kill you."

He chuckled at her teasing, the first he'd heard from her lips. He liked it.

"Let me see to breakfast and refresh your poultice. You must be hungry since you skipped supper yesterday."

"Did I now? I don't remember."

"Yes, well, I doubt you remember much after lunch."

She might be right, but he remembered waking to her head beside him. He wouldn't be forgetting that memory anytime soon, and he wanted it again.

Ellie awoke, and Anna fed her while Levi ate. When the child finished, she stretched out her arms wanting to come to Levi. He put out his arms to receive her. "How old is Ellie?"

"She's a little over ten months old. She was born in January, two months early. For a while, we feared she wouldn't make it, but she did."

That would be the reason Ellie appeared younger, but she must be tenacious like her mother. Something told him that Anna had learned to be a survivor long ago.

Anna left Ellie on the bed while she changed his bandage. When she unwrapped the old one, he heard her suck in her breath. He could smell the rotten odor and knew what it must look like. "Is it bad?"

"I'm hoping it's not as bad as it looks. Hopefully, the poultice is drawing out the infection like it's supposed to." Her face didn't look hopeful, however. "I need you to drink a full cup of willow bark tea."

He could do that. She added honey to it, and, although somewhat bitter, he could tolerate it fine.

Midmorning, Anna put Ellie down for a nap. "Come sit with me for a while if you will," he told Anna when she came from the bedroom. "I guess all the sleeping I've done lately has left me more awake than usual."

She hesitated, and her brow wrinkled. "You still need your rest to recover, and I need to wash some diapers."

"Then maybe a long conversation will make me sleepy."

She smiled. "Are you saying a conversation with me will be boring?" But she moved toward the chair at his bedside.

"Nothing of the sort, but I do tire easily now."

Her smile quickly faded, and, he wanted it back, but the things he wanted to know might not encourage a smile. "Tell me about your childhood and the orphan house."

She proceeded to do so. Reading between the lines, he saw the lack of attention or love, and his heart went out to her. Maybe that's why she took extra effort to see that Ellie received special attention and care.

"How did you meet your husband?"

She shook her head, but her eyes danced in amusement. "No, for every question I answer, you must answer one of mine. Did you grow up here in the mountains?"

He told her about moving here and why. Her teeth worried with her bottom lip as he explained about Leanore, his aversion to her brazenness, and the trouble it caused with T.J. If that part of his story bothered her, he'd better not share the part about Violet right now.

He restated his question, and her face fell even farther as she told him about Elbert and his father coming to the orphan house and interviewing the older girls for a wife. According to what she said, neither one of them was in love at the wedding. However, he had heard of many cases where arranged marriages ended in love. Had hers? He couldn't tell from what she said or from her expressions.

"Elbert said he chose me that day because of my looks. His father would have preferred one of the others." She looked down at her hands in her lap. "I've come to realize comeliness can be as much of a curse as a blessing."

He could agree with that, but did it mean she'd never developed feelings for her husband or that he'd never fallen in love with her? Levi didn't know how to ask such a personal question without upsetting her. He couldn't imagine a man living with this woman and not loving her, though.

"Why did you agree to marry a man you didn't know?"

"I had little choice." Her eyes pleaded with him to understand. "I had hoped to be accepted into teacher training, but they already had all the students they would take. Marriage seemed a better option than what might have happened to me once I had to leave the orphan house. I had already turned eighteen and could no longer stay."

"Was your husband good to you?"

"Yes. He treated me well." Her demeanor made Levi think she hadn't told him everything, but he knew he'd asked too many personal questions already.

Anna seemed to realize the conversation had become too probing, because she changed the subject. "I can't believe how easily Ellie has taken to you. You're good with her."

"She's a little sweetheart, and she's probably missing her father."

He could kick himself for adding that last part when he saw the cloud that came across Anna's face. Did she miss her husband that much? Of course she did.

"I doubt it." She wouldn't look at Levi. "Elbert and his father were disappointed Ellie wasn't a boy. He didn't show his daughter much attention."

"That's a shame."

"I named her Ellie after him, hoping that would help. It didn't." She looked around, apparently tiring of the conversation. "I'd better get some chores done. We can talk more, later."

"I hope so."

Levi could tell his temperature had returned that afternoon. Anna changed his bandage again and gave him more willow bark tea, but his leg ached and felt tight, and his headache had returned, too.

Anna must have noticed his discomfort, for she came and touched his head. If she would just keep holding her hand there, it would make him feel better. "Your fever is up again."

She had him drink some more willow bark tea and washed his face with cool water. The last thing he remembered was her touch.

Chapter Eight: Critical

Anna unwrapped Levi's bandage with trembling hands. The unconscious man moaned when she pressed on his leg to force more of the pus out, and the odor sickened her. What could she do to help him?

She decided to remove the stitches to see if that would help. Maybe it would let the pus drain out better and enable the poultice to do a more thorough job. She wished she had better medicines. She had heard of people years ago using maggots to eat away the pus and infected flesh, a disgusting thought, but she might have even tried that if any flies or maggots could be found in the freezing cold of a mountain winter.

Cutting the threads and getting the stitches pulled out took some time. Afterwards, she got a basin of warm water and washed the area thoroughly. The gash didn't gap as much as it had when she'd stitched it together, so some healing had taken place. She checked his leg for signs of discoloration, a sign of gangrene, but she couldn't be sure. The whole swollen leg looked so inflamed and red, but she could detect no greenish tint or darkening.

This time, she heated the new poultice, thinking the warmth might help it draw, although she took care not to cook the vegetables. By the time she'd rebandaged the wound, Levi had become restless and delirious.

"Anna." His voice sounded so weak she barely caught the word. "Anna?"

"Yes, I'm here."

"Stay." He reached for her without opening his eyes.

She put her hand in his hot one, wanting to give him whatever strength and comfort she could. The act drew her to him, as if they connected in a special way.

She pulled away. "I'll get you a cold cloth for your head and some more willow bark tea." She didn't know if he could hear her, but she'd talk to him just in case.

Throughout the day, Anna spooned willow bark tea into him, changed his poultice twice more, and tried to keep him comfortable. He alternated between taking chills and sweating. After he sweated, his fever always seemed to abate somewhat, but it never left him completely. Each time she changed the bandage, she cleaned his leg and wound, but the putrid smell grew stronger.

That night she sat beside his bed, afraid to leave him alone. He needed more care than she knew how to give, but she would do everything she could to help him fight the infection and fever. She had heard that once the infection set in the consequences were always dire, but she would not give up, not as long as he had a breath left in him.

Sometime after midnight, he became more restless. "No, Violet! I will not marry you. We have nothing in common."

How many women had chased after him? It's a wonder someone hadn't caught him. Well, she wouldn't be one of them. She never wanted another loveless marriage. She and Ellie would make it some way. With God's help.

The following day brought more to do than Anna could get done. With Levi still unconscious, no one played with Ellie, and both she and Levi needed attention. When Ellie took her naps, Anna had time to do the outside chores and get a few things done inside, but she would have liked a nap herself. Since she had gotten little sleep the night before, it felt like a long day.

She changed Levi's bed by rolling him to one side and then the other. He had taken care of his personal needs with a chamber pot before, but now he wet the bed. However, his body must be using much of the small amount of liquid she managed to get in him, because it didn't happen often. However, the sheets would have to be washed, adding to her tasks. She wished she could also remove his pants, but she dared not. At least they didn't appear to still be wet like the bed. It took some time to complete the task, but Levi didn't try to fight her when she rolled him around.

The night didn't change much from the night before, although Levi didn't call out any. Anna began by sitting beside his bed, but she startled awake with her head resting on the bed to find him burning up and thrashing about.

"Lord, help me. I'm afraid I'm losing Levi. Please show me what to do so he'll recover. He seems like a good man, committed to you, but if it's Thy will to take him, then take him quickly without much suffering or pain." She wiped the tears out of her eyes.

She made the willow bark tea stronger yet, and used a cool cloth on his head while it cooled. Then, she sat beside him on the bed, put a towel under his chin, raised his head, and tried to pour some of the tea into him. Remarkably, he drank much of it, only spilling a little.

In about half an hour, he began to sweat, and she bathed him in cool water, reaching all the places she dared to touch. When he appeared to rest better, she pulled all the covers up again.

Feeling as if she couldn't hold her head up any longer, Anna headed to sleep beside Ellie. Morning would come soon, and she had done all she could for Levi. She must leave him in God's hands now.

Anna gave Levi some more of the medicinal tea first thing the next morning. She couldn't tell if he had improved or not, but he still lived.

Since Levi wouldn't be drinking any, she decided not to make coffee just for her. She wanted to conserve her supply, although, with the two Ramsey men gone, it would last longer than usual. Still, she had no idea how she would get the things she needed, like flour, sugar, and coffee. She didn't even know where to take the corn to be ground into cornmeal or how much corn she would be able to raise by herself in the coming year.

She shook her head. She shouldn't let her mind run on so. Instead, she needed to take each day as it came. She could try to make other plans when spring came.

She had enough eggs to cook for breakfast, and perhaps she could get Levi to swallow some if she soft-scrambled them. He hadn't eaten anything at all yesterday, and he needed strength to fight the infection.

If he ate the eggs, she still had a few limp greens in the root cellar she'd been trying to save to have later. She found she could keep them there for a couple of months. Mrs. Bull thought they promoted good health, and she forced the orphans to eat them at least twice a month. Anna would probably have enough to feed Levi some and still have a mess left for later.

She got about one egg into Levi, although she had to coax him to swallow by rubbing underneath his chin. When she changed his bandage and applied a fresh poultice, she thought the wound look slightly less red or swollen, but it was difficult to tell. Perhaps she just saw what she wanted to see. At least she could still detect no darkening of the skin and flesh, so she should take hope in that.

Levi remained unconscious all day, but his fever didn't soar as high as it had, although he remained too warm to her touch, even with the willow bark tea. Anna remained just as vigilant, afraid that he would regress if she didn't keep up the established regiment.

Ellie became fussy, and Anna feared she might be getting sick. She held her in the chair beside Levi's bed until the little girl fell asleep, and then she put her beside Levi. That way she could watch them both at the same time.

While they slept, she managed to get the laundry done. If Levi woke up, she would get him some of Elbert's clean clothes to put on, but she dared not try to change him now. No, not *if* he woke up but *when*. She would not let defeat take root.

Ellie woke up and began to chew on her fingers. Now that Anna thought about it, she had been drooling more than usual and must be teething. She felt in her daughter's mouth, and, sure enough, she felt the beginnings of a new tooth. She would rub a little tincture of chamomile on it. She had dried some to use for this.

Come to think of it, she could use some on Levi's wound, too, once the poultice was no longer needed to draw out the pus. People used an ointment made from the herb for insect bites and on wounds.

With the chamomile helping to ease the soreness in her gums and a little weak willow bark tea to help with the pain, Ellie went to sleep without any problem. Anna carried her to the back bedroom and tucked her in. She'd leave the door open as she'd been doing, but she knew she'd have to sit beside Levi again tonight.

"No-o-o!" The scream jerked Anna awake, and it felt like her heart stopped for a second. Levi started throwing his arms around, as if he were fighting off demons. When he also started kicking, she became afraid he would further injure his leg.

"Sh-h-h. It's all right." She tried to calm him. She took his hands, but he pulled them away and continued to thrash about.

When she saw a long cut on his face from where he'd scratched himself with his flailing, she crawled onto the bed and wrapped an arm around his, hoping to prevent him from injuring himself, but he fought against her, and she didn't think she could hold him down. Even in his weakened state, he was strong.

"Levi, everything's fine. Please stop fighting me." He stopped pushing against her arm.

She leaned in close to his ear and whispered, "You're going to be all right. Do you hear me? I'm taking care of you, and together we're going to beat this infection. But I need for you to calm down, so I can help you."

He gave a sigh. "Anna?"

"Yes, it's me. It's Anna." She could have sworn his lips moved to a slight smile, but it vanished too quickly to be sure.

When she changed his bandage the next morning, she didn't find as much pus as usual, and the rotten odor didn't smell as pronounced. His forehead felt some cooler, too, but he never had as much fever in the morning. Whether or not it would stay down in the evening would be the test.

He didn't wake up for the rest of the day, but he didn't become so restless again, either. Even in the evening, chills didn't rack his body nor did he break out in a sweat. *Lord, please let this mean he's on the mend.*

Anna debated on whether to go to bed with Ellie or sit beside Levi again. She finally decided to sit up. She wanted to do everything she could to prevent another turn for the worse. When he became conscious again, she would go back to her own bed.

Levi came awake slowly. It took a moment to understand where he was, but when he saw Anna with her head on the bed, he remembered. He recalled bits and pieces of her taking care of him. He must have been pretty sick.

A tickle in his throat caused him to cough, and Anna jerked her head up from the bed. The dark circles under her eyes and haggard appearance told a story he didn't want to hear.

"You're awake."

"I am." He wanted to take her in his arms and comfort her. "How long have I been asleep?"

"You've been unconscious for several days. How do you feel?"

"Several days?" Had she been trying to sit up with him all that time?

She nodded. "I thought we were going to lose you there for a while. You've been very sick."

"And you've been tending me the whole time. I'm sorry to put you through that."

"I'm just glad you're on the mend." She stood. "You need your rest, too, or else you'll get sick."

"I'll be fine."

"You look tired and worn out."

"Gee, thanks." She absentmindedly tried to smooth her hair. "That's what every woman wants to hear."

He smiled. She had never come so close to flirting before. "Anna, you'd be beautiful no matter what, but I don't like seeing you so exhausted, and I know I'm the cause."

She looked away. "I wasn't fishing for a compliment."

"I know, but it's true just the same."

Without another word, she turned and went to stoke the fire. Perhaps he shouldn't have mentioned her beauty. Hadn't she said she considered it a curse, and did she think that's all he saw in her? He needed to take things slower and be careful with what he said. He could tell she wasn't ready for anything that bordered on courting.

She went about preparing breakfast. When she helped prop him up in bed and handed him his food, her face softened. "I'm glad you can sit up and eat this morning."

Maybe she wasn't too upset with his remark about her beauty. He reached to take her hand, but she jerked it away before he could catch it. "Thank you for taking such good care of me and nursing me back to health."

She took a step back. "You've not fully recovered yet. Your leg still needs to heal."

"But I still appreciate all you've done and all you will do."

Ellie cried out from the bedroom, and Anna went to collect her daughter. "You're welcome," she called over her shoulder.

She fed Ellie and sat her on a quilt in the floor with some things to play with. While Anna worked in the kitchen, Ellie looked over at Levi, gave a big grin, and crawled toward the bed. When she got there, she sat up and looked confused for a moment. Then, she took hold of the covers and pulled herself up.

By that time, Anna had spotted her. "Ellie, you're standing on your own!"

Startled by her mother's exclamation, Ellie fell back to a sitting position and puckered up to cry. Anna came quickly. "It's all right, darling." She picked Ellie up, and the little girl leaned for Levi.

Anna looked at him. "Do you feel like watching her for a while? I haven't milked yet."

He put out his hands. "I'd be glad to." He truly liked entertaining the child. When she started babbling, he decided to tell her some words. He began by showing her his hand and naming it, and then he did the same to hers. He pointed to himself and said "Levi."

She said something that almost sounded like "da-da," and he smiled.

"I'd like to be your daddy." He hugged her to him at the thought.

She willingly leaned into his chest, and the sweet moment almost brought tears to his eyes. When had he gotten so emotional?

Anna walked in. He pointed to her and said "Mama." Ellie looked but didn't try to make the sounds.

Anna sat the milk bucket and basket on the table and came toward them. "Is Levi teaching you to talk this morning?"

Afraid that Anna would take her, Ellie leaned into Levi again. "Come on now, "Anna told her as she picked her up. "You mustn't wear Levi out. He needs to rest."

"She's a sweetheart, and I enjoy her company."
However, he did feel weak and exhausted. Apparently, his unconscious bout had sapped much of his strength.

So many emotions moved across Anna's face, he could begin to name them all – perhaps regret, longing, surprise, and others. He couldn't be sure.

She looked at him. "Nap for a while. You look tired, and you need plenty of rest."

He refrained from teasing her about those being words no man wanted to hear, but couldn't keep from saying, "You do, too, Anna. Please take a nap this morning when Ellie does."

She smiled but didn't agree. At least his comment hadn't insulted her this time. Or had she been teasing before?

Levi woke up to Ellie's fuss as Anna wiped her up from dinner. "Did you get a nap?" he asked Anna.

"Yes, I managed a short one. Let me get you some stew."

After she handed him the food, she felt his forehead and frowned. You're getting warmer. I'll make some more willow bark tea for you. You haven't had any since breakfast."

He loved her touch and would have liked to grab her hand to prevent her moving it, but he reminded himself to take things slowly. She acted as skittish of his attention as a bug trapped in a spider's web.

He'd eaten, and Anna had just cleaned up the kitchen when they heard a loud knock at the door. Anna sucked in her breath and stood stock still. The pounding came again.

She grabbed the gun she carried with her when she went outside and opened the door. "Howdy, ma'am." A man's voice. "Me and Clem come to check on ya and see if'n you thought on hitchin' up."

Anna closed the door, probably to keep the men from seeing Levi, but he could still hear them. "My answer to that will stay the same, Mr. Hicks. I will not marry either pne of you."

"Now, none of that 'Mr. Hicks' stuff. Hit's plain ole Orin and Clem. And you'd better thank on that agin. You ain't goin' to be able to make hit stuck up here all by yourself."

"My daughter and I are making it just fine. Now, if you'll excuse me, I need to see to Ellie."

It sounded as if Anna took hold of the door, but then she said, "Stop right there!"

"Thar's more'n one way to skin a bobcat. Let me show you what you're missin'."

Levi got out of bed quickly, trying his best not to put any weight on his leg as he took the crutch Anna had leaned against the wall. Then, he headed for his rifle hanging on pegs beside the front door.

"I will shoot you Mr. Hicks, and from this range, I'm not going to miss."

"You ain't goin' kill me, now."

"I hope not, but I will do what it takes to protect myself and my daughter. You've just shown me what kind of men you are, and God will see that you're punished for this."

"Don't be brangin' God into this."

"God is in everything, whether or not you recognize it."

Levi moved to the window where he could see Anna, but he stood back at an angle where he hoped the men wouldn't see him. All their attention seemed to be fixed on Anna, who held the gun steadily pointed at the chest of the man who called himself "Orin."

Levi leveled his rifle on Clem, but he'd be able to quickly fire on either one. He thought about going out and standing beside her, but he knew she'd be furious if he did, because her reputation would be ruined. No, he'd wait here for now. He didn't want to bring her any more trouble than his accident already had.

Chapter Nine: Tension

"All right, all right." Orin put up his hands, but Anna took a step back, leaning against the door. Now Orin couldn't reach to jerk the rifle out of her hands before she could get a shot off. "I jist wanted to give you a little kiss. Nothin' wrong with that. We'll be goin' fer now, but don't thank this is the last of hit."

Anna rushed into the cabin, shut the door, and closed her eyes.

"You handled that well."

Her eyes flashed open. "What are you doing out of bed?"

"I wasn't going to let anything happen to you."

"As you said, I had everything under control. Now get back to bed. I don't want you putting stress on that leg until it heals. I've worked too hard to save you to have you rip it open or cause another infection."

"Yes, ma'am." He put his gun back on the pegs and worked hard not to let his amusement show. He even held his head down as he maneuvered back to the bed. She just looked so cute, spitting commands like that. He really wanted to take her in his arms and kiss her, but he tried to wipe those thoughts from his mind. He knew, if he did, he'd ruin everything.

"Are the Hicks brothers the reason you always carry the rifle with you when you go outside?" Levi asked her after supper.

Worry lines riveted her forehead. "They're part of the reason. I just wish they'd leave me alone. After that mountain lion killed Elbert, I also decided it would be better for me to be able to protect myself."

"I take it Orin and Clem have been here before."

"Yes, one other time. They said they wanted me to marry one of them. I could have my pick, but Orin suggested him, since he's the oldest."

The thought of Anna marrying one of those scraggly men made Levi's skin crawl. "You shouldn't have to fend off the likes of them, and you won't have to if they come back again. I'll take care of them."

"No you won't!" She put her hand over her mouth, as if surprised by her own outburst. "I mean, I hope you won't do anything rash. If people know that you've been staying with me, they'll get the wrong idea, and the fact that I've been tending to you in sickness won't make any difference."

"I sure don't want to cause you any trouble, but I won't stay back and do nothing while they threaten or terrorize you."

"Please let me handle things. You'll be leaving as soon as you're healed, so you won't always be here to help. I need to be able to take care of me and Ellie myself."

It galled him to think of her and Ellie living in this remote cabin all alone. He didn't see how she'd be able to do everything herself, even if the Hicks brothers didn't pester her. How would she even get enough firewood cut for next winter and take care of Ellie and the farm? He vowed that even if she never wanted him in her life, he'd see to it that she had enough to survive.

"Are you planning to stay here alone then?" He had to ask.

She looked away. "For now, but I don't know about later on. I've not decided what's best yet, and I'm hoping God will show me. Do you know of any positions around that I might find enough work to support Ellie and me? Maybe a job as a cook, housekeeper, nanny, or even a schoolteacher or such."

"I don't, but I've not been here all that long myself. I'll ask my brother, though. He knows the area better."

Even thinking of her working for someone didn't sit well with him. If he could ask her to marry him and she accepted, it would solve her problems, but he didn't know if either one of them was ready for that at this point. Although he liked what he'd seen and felt drawn to her, he needed to get to know her better. And, after the way the Hicks brothers were trying to force her into marriage and the recent death of her husband, she needed time. By what she'd told him, circumstances and the director of the orphan house in Charleston had pressured her into marrying Elbert. He didn't think she'd take kindly to anyone else trying to rush her.

He'd love to court her, however. Yet he knew she'd reject that, too. She needed time. He remembered what his mother once told him. "It sometimes takes time, right conditions, and the correct handling to get cream to rise to the top or to bring out the best in someone." He'd have to keep reminding himself of that over and over again, because when it came to Anna, he'd become more impatient than he'd ever known himself to be.

Levi watched Anna go about her tasks for the next few days. The Hicks brothers had left a dark cloud over her, and a tension that hadn't been there before permeated the cabin like the heavy, charged air before a storm.

Ellie became their bright spot. Levi looked forward to playing with her, and it allowed Anna to go about her chores unimpeded.

The girl had started saying "da-da" more and more around him, but she often chattered her baby talk, and he didn't think anything about it. He continued to name objects and sometimes he thought she tried to repeat them, but the words didn't sound similar, and he couldn't be sure.

Anna came to get Ellie to feed her lunch, but Ellie shook her head and snuggled into Levi. Anna gave him a hard look.

"Come on, Ellie. It's time to eat. After your nap, you can come back and play with Levi." Anna pulled her away from Levi.

"Da-da," Ellie fussed. "Da-da, da-da!"

Anna froze. "Why is she calling you 'daddy' now? Why is that the first word she's saying? Did you teach her to say it?"

"No. I've heard her say the sounds, but I had no idea she meant me. I haven't taught her to say it."

Anna rubbed her daughter's back to soothe her. "I'm not sure you showing Ellie so much attention is a good thing. What will she think when you leave and never come back?"

"I can come back. I'll come back to visit." In fact, he wanted a reason to visit as often as possible. He just hoped this farm wasn't too far from his brother's place. He'd become so disoriented in the blizzard that he had no idea where he'd come.

Anna looked at him with doubt written on her face. Didn't she believe him?

"I promise you I didn't teach her to say 'daddy.'"

Anna nodded, as if she chose to believe him for now. "I just want to protect her. She's already lost her father, and she's closer to you than to him."

"I want to protect her, too." In fact, he wanted to protect both of them. "I'd never willingly do anything to hurt her."

Anna's eyes softened. "I know you wouldn't."

"Could I get up and sit in a chair for a while?" Levi asked Anna the next morning. "I feel as if I'm growing to this bed."

She smiled. Oh, but if only he could keep such a smile on her face. "Let me bring you some clean clothes and a basin of water first. Ellie and I will stay in the bedroom while you wash up and change clothes. We'll see if you still feel like sitting up after that."

Anna would have made a good prophetess. By the time he'd finished bathing and changing clothes, he felt as if he'd done a hard day's manual labor.

"I can tell you're exhausted," Anna said when she came to pick up the dirty clothes and basin.

He nodded and closed his eyes. "Maybe I can stay out of bed for a while in the morning."

"If you feel like it, you can come to the table to eat your breakfast." He felt her pull his covers tighter around his shoulders. It felt good to be pampered.

Anna stopped dicing the potatoes and just watched Levi sleep for a minute. She still didn't trust him, because he seemed too nice, too sweet. No man of her acquaintance acted like him. Not only had he arose from his sickbed to protect her, but he acted as if he liked having Ellie around. At times his look made Anna want to melt into his arms, and that scared her most of all. After having a marriage that stretched far from her ideal, she didn't want to be dependent on another man. She wanted to make it on her own.

Mrs. Bull would have been appalled at such a thought. No woman in her right mind would seek independence, for it would just be asking for trouble. But her marriage had taught her that she'd be better off alone than with a cold, withdrawn husband or a husband that only loved her looks.

Levi turned over, and a lock of dark hair fell across his forehead. She bit her lip to stop herself from going over and brushing it from his face. What a contradiction! On one hand, she wanted to stay far from the man, but on the other hand, something about him drew her.

When Levi got up the next morning and hobbled to the table for breakfast with his crutch, Anna sucked in her breath. This had too much of a family feel to it, something that she longed for, but not with just anyone.

Ellie didn't hide her joy but had to sit on Levi's lap to eat. He smiled sweetly at the little girl and didn't complain about feeding her.

Ellie looked up at him with her mouth filled with mush and mumbled, "Da-da." Then she looked over at Anna, pointed her finger, and said "Ma-ma."

Anna didn't know what to say, so she tried to ignore her daughter's words. She didn't want to argue with Levi over it again, and she didn't want to scold Ellie for trying to talk.

She had feared Ellie might be behind other children her age due to her early birth and sickly start. The fact that she could now pull up to stand and had begun to assign words to objects relieved the worry about Ellie's progress, and she knew that she had Levi to thank for much of it. How could she reprimand them?

After he'd eaten, Levi sat at the table while she cleaned up and washed the dishes. He put Ellie down but held to her as she took a few steps around the front of his chair.

When Anna had finished, she had Levi go back to bed and put Ellie on it with him. She needed to do the outside chores, and she knew Levi would likely tire before she got back if he remained sitting up.

Christmas would be here soon, and Anna needed to get busy making some gifts. At the orphan house, some charitable patrons usually donated enough that each child could at least have a piece of candy and sometimes an orange as well. She wanted Ellie to have more, and this would be her first Christmas.

She'd already started making Ellie a rag doll. She had embroidered the face and knotted the yarn hair in before she sewed the body parts together and stuffed them. Anna wanted to make it durable, even for a one-year-old girl. Now she just needed to make its dress.

She also wanted to make something for Levi, but she had no idea what. She didn't have enough new cloth to make him any clothing, but perhaps she could find something usable from Mr. Ramsey's clothes. She hesitated to use Elbert's for a gift to Levi, but she would if that's all she had. She didn't know why that would matter to her anyway and wondered if it would matter to Levi.

While Ellie and Levi took a nap, Anna rummaged through Mr. Ramsey's old trunk to try to find something she could use to make Levi a gift. Near the bottom she found a new looking shirt out of a superior grade of cotton. It would be way too small for Levi, but she could cut it up to make a set of nice handkerchiefs, and she could embroider his initials in the corner of each.

When she lifted the shirt out, she saw a small leather bag in the bottom of the trunk. Curious, she pulled it out and opened it. Inside she found ten twenty-dollar gold pieces, surely a fortune.

If Mr. Ramsey had this much money, why did he live so meagerly and regret every penny spent? She took out one coin and slipped it in her pocket, but put the rest back where she found them. *Thank you, Lord.* This would go a long way in providing for her and Ellie.

Levi became able to stay up for longer periods of time. "Could we read the Bible and pray together in the evenings before we go to bed?" he asked one night.

"I try to find time to do that sometime during each day, but it would be good to have a set time." She didn't know about having a devotion with Levi, however.

"We'll share doing it," he said. "I'll choose the Bible verses and say the prayer tonight, and you can do it tomorrow night. If you want to discuss it, we can do that, too."

"Anna, do you think you can find me some pieces of wood big enough to carve Ellie a toy for Christmas? Pine or some softer wood would work better."

"You don't need to give her anything. She's so young, she'll be happy with getting the doll I'm making her."

"I'll know." His eyes pleaded with her. "I want to make her something."

She nodded. "I should be able to find something among the firewood, although most of it is hardwood."

"My carving is going to make a mess on your floor," he told her as he pulled out his knife to begin.

It amazed her that he would care. Elbert and Mr. Ramsey wouldn't have. "Don't worry about it. If you pull your chair up close to the fireplace, I can just sweep what falls across the hearth into the fire."

"I'll throw the larger hunks in as I go."

"What are you going to make?"

"I'm not sure yet. Some kind of animal, I suppose, but I'll let the wood show me what would be best."

Anna wanted to stand and watch him carve, but she knew she shouldn't. She tried to get a glimpse of his work, but she couldn't get enough details in a quick glance to determine what it would turn out to be. Only after it neared completion did she recognize a rabbit, which would be the size of a baby one.

By the week before Christmas, Levi sat up more than he stayed in the bed during the day. He had started taking naps when Ellie did, but that's all. Somehow, Ellie had begun taking her nap on Levi's bed, and she seemed to rest longer there with him.

However, Ellie went to bed at night earlier than Levi, and Anna insisted she use the bedroom then. She needed her daughter snuggled beside her when she retired for the night.

Those times with just the two of them, when Levi pulled his chair close to the fire for the light to whittle by and Anna sat on the other side of the fireplace sewing, made her uncomfortable. The peace of the moment warmed her heart and felt so right that it scared her to death. She couldn't let Levi inch his way into her heart. She dared not. He would be leaving soon.

"I'm going out to gather some greenery to decorate for Christmas," she told Levi when Ellie was down for her nap.

"Let me come, too." His eyes pleaded with her. "I'm an outdoors person, and staying cooped up this long is about to kill me."

"Just a little longer. Your leg needs to heal enough that you can put weight on it."

"But I don't like you roaming around out there. The Hicks brothers could take you by surprise."

"I'll hardly need to leave the yard. There's a large holly bush just in back of the barn, and I'll cut a few evergreen branches. That's all. Besides, I need you to stay with Ellie."

"Be careful, then. Please." The intensity of emotion in his eyes made her look away.

She hurried to collect what she needed, and made it back to the cabin within thirty minutes. She didn't understand the look of relief on Levi's face.

She had a good time spreading the branches around the cabin. She put some on each window sill and on the mantel. She even covered the trunk in her room with them, because she liked the smell so much.

She wished she had some red ribbons to add to them, but she didn't. She didn't even have any red cloth or she could have made some bows. But she did like the fragrance that smelled like Christmas, and the holly boughs gave the decorations a touch of red.

"I like what you've done to decorate." Levi nodded at the mantle.

"Thank you. Sometimes someone would donate a tree at the orphan house, and we had fun decorating it, but I knew that would be too big a task for this year. Maybe I can have at least a small one when Ellie is old enough to really enjoy it."

Anna woke up on Christmas Eve to snow but no wind blew. Instead of a blizzard, large, fluffy flakes fell to create a white wonderland. Levi got up soon after her and joined her at the window. "It's beautiful, isn't it?" she whispered.

"Yes, it is." But when she looked at him, he stood much too close, and his eyes were on her.

"It's colder out there than it looks." Anna took off her wraps near the back door and tried to stomp the snow off her shoes before she tracked through the house. "I'm chilled to the bone."

"Let me start milking and doing the outside chores for you," Levi responded immediately. "I can get around well enough now."

She walked to stand in front of the fireplace for its warmth. "Absolutely not. It's slick out there, and if you fell, who knows what kind of damage you'd do to that leg."

"Then after the snow's gone."

"We'll see."

"You're quite bossy, aren't you?" His eyes danced with amusement, but he kept his lips from laughing, although she saw them twitch.

She didn't like being made a joke of when she had worked so hard to get him well. She just wanted to keep him on the mend.

But then he turned serious. "If I wanted to go outside, I doubt if you could stop me short of shooting me in the back, but because I respect you, I choose to listen to your advice. I know you're concerned about my welfare and have put much effort into getting me well. I appreciate all that you've done."

She didn't know what to say, so she remained quiet. She turned to straighten his bed, but he'd already made it up.

"Now, what can I do to help you in the house? At least let me help here where it's not slick and I'm not apt to fall." His eyes sparkled in merriment again.

Anna didn't quite know how to take Levi's teasing. Elbert had been so withdrawn from her most of the time. Until he wanted something from her, he often acted almost as if she didn't exist.

Just the opposite, Levi demanded attention. Even when he remained quiet and not teasing, he noticed her, and she stayed constantly aware of him. He filled the cabin by just being there, and she felt she could never escape him. Even when he slept, she felt his presence and found herself watching him or glancing his way all too often.

Chapter Ten: Christmas and Beyond

Christmas Day turned out to be clear, although snow still covered the ground. Anna got up early and slipped out to the barn. She wanted to get the outside chores done early, so she'd be inside when Ellie and Levi got up. For some reason she couldn't fathom, she felt more excited about Christmas this year than any she could remember. It must be because of Ellie.

Anna made a large breakfast of biscuits, gravy, eggs, and sausage. She also set out the last of her apple butter, since it didn't keep as long as jams and preserves.

"Um-m-m. What wonderful smells to wake to," Levi said from the bed.

Ellie called "Ma-ma-ma" at the same time, so Anna went to the bedroom. By the time she changed Ellie, Levi would have had some time to himself to take care of his personal needs.

When she came back in carrying Ellie, Levi had moved to the table. "Here let me hold her while you get breakfast on the table."

Still sleepy, Ellie buried her head into Levi's shoulder. He rubbed her back and kissed her head. "Today's Christmas, Ellie. I think you might have some presents. Later on, I'll tell you all about Jesus' birth."

Ellie raised her head to get a better look at Levi. Anna had a feeling the child understood a lot more than they gave her credit for.

"I think I've eaten enough to do me the rest of the day," Levi teased. "It tasted too good to stop, but I don't want to eat you out of house and home."

"You'd better have saved room for dinner, too. I'm cooking a ham, and we'll have some vegetables and a dessert."

"I hate the thoughts of leaving your cooking behind, but please don't feel as if you have to do extra for me."

She couldn't tell if he teased again or had become serious. "I like to have someone enjoy my cooking. After all, we are celebrating Christmas, and I'm sure your sister-in-law feeds you."

"Not as well as you do. But I'm sure your family here has appreciated your cooking."

"If they have, they never said anything." The minute the words spilled from her lips, she wanted them back. The man didn't need to know everything about her life.

Levi looked at her as if he didn't know what to say, but his eyes softened. She looked away. She didn't want his pity. "Let me clean up here, and then we'll open presents." They needed to focus on something else.

Anna gave Ellie her ragdoll inside a pillowcase. She grinned when she saw it, and seemed delighted when she held it.

Levi had put the wood carving in the other pillow case. "It's a rabbit, Ellie," he told her. "Can you say "rab-bit?"

"Ra-ra, ra-ra," she repeated.

Anna handed Levi the handkerchiefs she'd made him. She'd rolled them together, and tied them with a piece of yarn. He truly looked surprised.

"These are wonderful, but you didn't need to give me anything. When did you even have time to work on them?"

"I have my ways."

He fingered the embroidery. She'd worked an "L" and a "W" in the corner of each white handkerchief with a different color thread on each one – black, brown, blue, and white.

He looked up. "A man can never get enough handkerchiefs. Thank you."

She tried to hide her smile, but couldn't. "You're welcome. I enjoyed making them." And she did.

He reached in his pocket, pulled out his old handkerchief Anna had just laundered, and handed it to her. "I made a little something for you, too."

She unwrapped it to find a small wooden cross. The elaborate carving and detail stunned her on such a small piece. "This is beautiful. Whenever did you do this?"

He grinned mischievously. "I have my ways. I carved a hole through the top, so you could use it on a necklace if you wanted."

"I have a black ribbon that will work for that just fine. Thank you. It's elegant and something I will treasure." The unexpected present touched her more than she dared say. How different this Christmas had turned out to be than the last one.

Ellie sat on her quilt and played with her toys for a long time. When she grew sleepy, Anna put her to bed for a nap. She went willing to the bedroom for a change, but she had to take her toys with her.

Levi didn't go to bed this time but continued to sit up. His presence unnerved her with the two of them alone without anything to divert their attention.

Anna moved to stoke the fire. "I'll make us some hot, spiced apple cider."

"That sounds good."

She could feel his eyes following her as she made their drink, but she tried not to meet his gaze. "We need to read the Christmas story from Luke this afternoon," she told him as she handed him his cup.

He nodded. "I want to."

She joined him at the table with her own cup of cider. "I need to start cooking, but I'll just drink this first."

"Sit with me a while first. I'm still full from breakfast." They sat in silence for a few minutes, and it didn't feel awkward. "Do you think my leg is going to heal so I can get around without problems? I'm trying to be patient, but it seems to be taking so long."

Was he in a big hurry to leave? She had thought she wanted him to go, but his leaving didn't seem to hold the appeal it once did. She worried less about her and Ellie's safety with him here. That's all it was.

"I don't know. It seems to be healing now, and there's no longer any infection, but it's hard to know how much damage you did and if the muscles or such will mend properly if you damaged them. You needed a surgeon, but I did what I could."

"I'm very thankful for what you've done. I know quite well that I would be dead if not for you. I'm just hoping that I won't walk with a heavy limp for the rest of my life. I don't want to be a burden to anyone, and I want to be able to do my share of the work."

Her heart went out to him for his concerns. "I know it must seem like slow progress to you, but you've made great progress. Give it time. I think you will continue to improve."

Dinner seemed as much a success as breakfast had, and they had plenty of food left for supper. Levi did take a nap when Ellie did that afternoon. After they both woke up, Levi played with Ellie for a while. Anna when out to milk right before supper, since it got dark so early now.

After supper, Levi read the Christmas story with Ellie sitting on his lap. The little girl must have liked the sound of his voice, because she sat still and listened. Anna liked the sound of his voice, too.

Before she went to bed for the night, Levi told Ellie the condensed, children's version of Jesus' birth. Ellie giggled and clapped her hands when he made the animal sounds that might have come from the stable.

"Thank you for a wonderful Christmas," Levi told her before they said good-night. "I don't remember having one any better."

"It's the best one I've ever had." The tender look Levi gave her let her know that she'd said too much again.

The snow finally left, and Levi insisted on doing the outside chores. Anna had to admit it eased her burdens more than she'd expected, but she wouldn't tell Levi that. The man had a stubborn streak when it came to helping her, so he took his crutch for support and went about milking, collecting the eggs, and feeding the animals.

When she looked out the back window and saw him take the axe and split the wood Elbert or Mr. Ramsey hadn't got to, she nearly screamed. She could envision the accident where his hatchet embedded into his leg.

She wanted to turn away and not watch, but she couldn't do that either. It reminded her of when Mr. Ramsey chopped the head off a rooster for her to clean and cook. The bizarre sight of the chicken flapping around with no head and splattering blood everywhere it went repelled but fascinated her at the same time.

She didn't want to see Levi get hurt, didn't want to think about it for that matter, but she felt compelled to watch and make sure he didn't. She whispered a prayer under her breath.

She watched him work, and breathed a sigh of relief when nothing disastrous happened. The chopping must have warmed him, because he took off his coat and laid it aside. His muscles rippled and strained against his shirt as he exerted himself, and Anna became acutely aware of his broad shoulders and strong arms. He didn't look at all bulky or large, but he did look fit and well-proportioned.

Compared with his father, Elbert had appeared stronger and better proportioned, but neither looked as good as Levi. She jerked away from the window. What was wrong with her? Sometimes, she just didn't understand herself and her wayward thoughts, but that hadn't been a problem before Levi came. He needed to find his way home. Soon.

Before Ellie's first birthday, Levi had quit using the crutch, although he still had a severe limp. Anna knew he'd been working in the barn on a birthday gift, but she had no idea what it could be since she didn't go to the barn anymore. When she asked, he smiled and said it was a surprise. Whatever it was, it took a lot of Levi's time.

Anna had made Ellie a new dress and her ragdoll one to match, and she planned to fix a special meal of Ellie's favorite foods. She had a choice between potato soup or chicken and dumplings. When she decided on chicken and dumplings, Levi killed and cleaned the chicken for her outside. Elbert would have never thought to do such a thing, and if he had, Mr. Ramsey would have ridiculed him over it.

Levi had been holding Ellie's hands and helping her walk around the cabin. He stooped over so much, Anna knew his back must be aching, but he never complained. She felt sure he'd have Ellie walking on her own soon.

The January day when Ellie turned one became bright and sunny after the morning haze burned off. It almost seemed like another Christmas as Anna went about trying to make the day special for her daughter. Ellie might not understand it all, but she laughed a lot and seemed to sense the excitement.

After they ate dinner, Anna cleaned Ellie up and brought out the new dress for her to wear. The pink calico suited her.

Levi went to the barn and came back carrying a wooden, rocking horse. Anna couldn't believe he'd made the impressive toy, and Ellie loved it. Levi held her on and showed her how to rock back and forth. It didn't take her long to catch on, and Anna felt her pride soar – pride in Ellie for being so precocious, but also pride in Levi and his talents. She mentally shook her head at herself. She had no right to feel pride in Levi; he wasn't hers in any way. *He's your friend.* Yes, maybe she could accept that. Levi West would make a good friend, but nothing more.

The days ran together in comfortable routine that Anna came to depend on. She found herself even depending on Levi, a fact that she had a hard time accepting, but he made life so much easier for her. Not only did he take care of many of the chores and enjoy tending to Ellie, but he provided a level of safety and security that she didn't feel on her own.

Levi cleared his throat, and Anna looked at him across the table from her. They'd finished their evening meal, Anna had put Ellie to bed, and she and Levi sat sipping some peppermint tea.

"Do you think it's time I thought about leaving?" He looked at her intently.

Why had he asked her such a question? She didn't want the decision of when he would leave. "I don't know? How does your leg feel?"

"It's gotten better all the time, although the progress is much slower than I'd like."

"Do you know where to go? Do you think you can find your way?" She didn't know why she hedged.

Hadn't she wished a hundred times that he would leave and quit working his way into her heart?

He gave her an indulgent smile. "I know I became disoriented in the blizzard, but I think I can eventually get to somewhere familiar if I head west. If I can't, I could find my way back here, since there'd be no storm."

She nodded. The lump in her stomach surprised her. She took another sip of her peppermint tea, which should be calming her stomach. "When were you thinking of leaving?"

"Day after tomorrow. My brother is likely worried and wondering if I'm still alive. I could return home and then come back to help you here if you wanted."

She tried to determine if that's what he wanted, but she couldn't tell by his expression. "No, it's best you go about your own life. So far, no one knows that I've had a man staying in the house for several months, and my reputation is intact. That won't be true indefinitely."

"Well, think on it. I could stay until the crops were in this spring."

She left his offer hanging. She'd like to have his help in the spring, but she dare not extend his stay that long. She'd started depending too much on him already, and she didn't want to be forced into that position ever again.

Two days later, they awoke to another blizzard, and the decision had been made for Anna. She didn't

know whether to rejoice or cry. Her feelings toward
Levi had become such a paradox. In some ways, she did
need him and longed for the comfort and security he
provided. In another way, he seemed too good to be true,
and the attraction she felt for him frightened her to the
core.

At times she wanted to run to his arms and
discover how his lips would feel on hers. At other times
she wanted to run as far from him as possible and never
see him again. He brought her peace and personal
turmoil all at the same time.

Levi stood in front of the window and watched the
wind beat the snow against the pane. The Ramseys had
done a decent job of building the cabin. Not every
mountain cabin had three glass windows, and the
chinking had held through the winter storms.

He thought back to when he'd told Anna he needed
to leave. He'd hoped beyond reason that she would ask
him to return, but he could tell by the look on her face
when he asked that she wouldn't. Yet she hadn't told
him to go and never come back. At least not this time.
The snowstorm had blown away her need to respond.

He wished he knew what made her so wary of him.
He'd picked up hints through their conversations that
her marriage hadn't turned out as she'd hoped, but he

didn't have much information. He did guess that her father-in-law had been a cold, harsh man. Hadn't Elbert stood up for his wife? Hadn't he been thrilled with the daughter she'd given him? From what he could gather, the man had done none of those things.

Ellie. Just thinking about the little girl brought a smile to his face. He couldn't imagine a sweeter, more delightful toddler. If only the mother would be as open and receptive as the daughter.

"I'm sorry you're not able to leave as planned."

He turned to face Anna, a much prettier sight than the view out the window. "I take it as a sign I'm supposed to stay for now."

A mixture of amusement and fear crossed Anna's face in that order. "Maybe so."

"At least I'm here to brave the elements and make it to the barn."

"For that I'm grateful."

"That I can understand." He tried to lighten the conversation. "One blast of that wind might carry such a petite woman away."

"I'm not all that petite." She bristled. "I happen to be five feet, four inches tall. That's not petite for a woman."

"It is next to my six-foot frame."

She gave a feminine snort. "I'd say that's about right for a man and a woman."

The retort seemed to shock her as much as it did him, but he couldn't contain the grin that spread over his face. "I'll agree with that."

Anna turned a delightful shade of rose. "Don't bait me, Levi. I don't appreciate it." She turned and stalked into her bedroom.

Levi walked over to the fireplace. He'd grown cold standing in front of the window, or was it Anna's coldness that chilled him? *Lord, please keep me from making matters worse between Anna and me.*

As Levi feared, a cold reserve hung between him and Anna as they sat in front of the fire that night. He read the Bible, or tried to, while Anna did some mending. She'd put Ellie to bed and sat in front of the fire for warmth and light, but he knew she'd rather be away from him. Should he apologize to her, even though he still meant what he'd said, or would bringing it up just freeze her more.

He turned his eyes on the page before him, and the verse in Ephesians 4:32 jumped out at him. After reading it to himself, he went back and read it aloud. "And be ye kind one to another, tenderhearted, forgiving one another, even as God for Christ's sake hath forgiven you."

He looked up at Anna. "I'm sorry if my impulsive remark made you uncomfortable, for that was not my intent. I just responded to what you'd said."

She colored again but not quite as profusely as she had before. "I hope you're not using the Bible for your personal advantage, Mr. West. But I accept your apology and also apologize for my improper remark."

He dared not tell her he didn't consider her statement improper at all, and he would love to hear more just like it. He nodded to keep from having to comment. After a long pause, he added, "Have you forgiven me enough to go back to calling me 'Levi' instead of 'Mr. West?'"

She didn't answer but asked a question of her own. "Will you leave as soon as the weather permits?"

"Do you want me to?"

She looked away from him. "I imagine that would be best."

Why did she try to slip from a direct answer? "But what do you want?"

"I don't know." She said it so softly he almost couldn't hear her, although she sat in a few feet of him. He could tell she'd given him the most honest answer she could, so he let it drop.

He knew he wanted her to end her reserve with him and let him get to know her. He knew he'd never been so interested in a woman before. Could it be because this one didn't run after him as so many others had?

The confused expression on her face spoke volumes. Perhaps she wasn't as indifferent to him as she tried to portray. Perhaps the fear he often saw in her eyes came from fighting her feelings for him. He needed to be patient with her, but his time here was running out.

Would he ever get to see her again after he left? He had a feeling she would tell him "no" if he asked.

Ellie had begun to walk on her own, and she had to be watched even closer than before. With two women in the house back at Noah's cabin, Levi hadn't realized how much attention a little one required. He tried to keep Ellie occupied and out of trouble as much as possible. At least the Ramseys had a fire screen to set in front of the fireplace when Anna wasn't cooking.

After the blizzard subsided, and the snow finally melted away, a cold spell hit with the days not warming above freezing and the nights plummeting to dangerously low levels. Even with a roaring fire, the cabin stayed so cold they needed more wraps if they didn't hover near the fireplace.

"Well, you certainly can't leave in this weather. If you had to stay out overnight, you'd freeze to death. In fact, I'd worry about you if you left before the end of March now."

Levi looked to see if he could detect how Anna felt about him being detained again, but she showed no emotion. However, he felt relief and hoped for a late spring.

Chapter Eleven: Spring

After deciding that Levi needed to stay until at least the end of March, Anna seemed to relax and grow more comfortable around him. Maybe having a definite time set eased her mind in some way. He hoped so.

Although March had some warmer days, it also had cold ones, and the wind often blew so fiercely it threatened to snatch anything in its path. Only with April, did spring look possible.

"I've stayed this long, so I'm going to see the garden plowed and ready for you to tend." Levi told Anna.

"You don't have to do that. I can manage."

"I don't want you to just manage, and this is something I can easily do for you. I just want to help and leave you and the farm in good shape. I can be stubborn, too." He smiled to keep from appearing too domineering.

"I think all men can be."

"Who's made you think so little of all men, Anna?"

She turned away without answering his question. "Very well. I'll accept your help and appreciate your thoughtfulness."

Levi worked the hardest he ever remembered, because he wanted to get as much done as possible before he left. And maybe he hoped she'd see how handy he'd be to have around. He plowed and broke up the large garden plot, and helped Anna put out an early crop of cabbage, onions, and potatoes. She could plant the rest of the garden come May or June.

He liked working beside her with Ellie playing nearby where they could watch her. They worked well together. Did she notice it, too?

He also cut and carried as much wood as he could, while Anna stacked it. They'd used most of what had been cut during the hard winter, and she would need some for cooking. He had time to get enough to do her through the summer, but he didn't know what she'd do next winter.

If the two cabins didn't stand a far distance apart, maybe he could come back and help her some more. Would she accept his help? Would she be glad to see him again?

Finally, he made repairs around the farm from damage done by the storms. Knowing that he'd taken care of as much as he could for now, he told Anna at supper that he'd leave in the morning. Although he

knew he needed to let Noah know he was all right, he
dreaded the thoughts of walking away.

Anna tried to swallow the lump in her throat when
Levi said he'd be leaving in the morning. Suddenly, her
food held no appeal. The man had managed to get way
too close to her despite all her resolve to not let him, and
the thought of never seeing him again stabbed her to the
quick.

He had done more work around the place in a few
weeks than Elbert and Mr. Ramsey would have done in
months. If judged by the pace at which the Levi worked,
one would think he couldn't wait to leave.

She almost shook her head at herself. She should
be thankful he had wanted to help her. She didn't know
what she would do come next winter, but she would
have it easier until then because of Levi.

Anna cooked a ham for supper the afternoon
before Levi planned to leave. She'd have enough left to
use in a hearty breakfast in the morning, and she could
make some ham biscuits for him to take with him.

Despite how much she'd given herself a talking-to,
gloom hung over her. She'd told herself over and over
he needed to leave, and she believed it, but her heart still
didn't want him to go. She'd cautioned herself many
times not to come to depend on him, but she had.

Lord, what am I going to do without him?

After Ellie went to bed, she and Levi sat before the fire as they had so many times before. He didn't appear to want to go to bed tonight any more than she did.

"I can come back after I let my family know I'm all right." He looked hopeful, wanting her to tell him that would be fine.

She couldn't. "That would just mean parting again. No, you have your life, and I have mine."

"It doesn't have to be that way."

She knew he hinted that he'd like to stay permanently, but to his credit, he didn't try to push her. Did he want to marry her? It wouldn't be right to stay together indefinitely without it, even with their platonic relationship continuing.

Although they'd lived in the same cabin for over four months, she still didn't feel like she knew Levi well. Oh, she knew him to be a good, honest man, but then so was Elbert. They hadn't talked about personal things, like hopes and dreams. She didn't know most of his favorite things or how he'd treat her in a closer relationship, because she'd tried to keep him at arm's length. No, she wasn't ready for marriage and didn't know if she would ever be.

Levi lingered over the breakfast that had been more like a feast. Anna had done her best to make his last meal here special. He'd like to think that meant she cared for him, but he knew better. She just had a kind nature. Otherwise, she'd never taken him in and nursed him back to health.

He had his few belongings packed, including the food Anna wanted to send with him. Now he just needed to tell Anna and Ellie good-bye and walk away. Walking away had become a mountain that would be almost impossible to climb.

He picked Ellie up and hugged her to him. She put her arms around his neck and buried her face into his shoulder. He rubbed her back. "You be a good girl for Mama and remember I love you."

She lifted her head and patted his cheek with her little hand. "Da-da."

He sat her down and turned to Anna. "I'll miss you."

She nodded.

He opened his arms. "Could I get a good-bye hug?"

She hesitated only a moment before she stepped into his arms. He held her there, trying not to squeeze her too tightly, although he wanted to hang on to her with all his might.

"You take care of yourself and Ellie. I'll be praying for you," he whispered.

"I'll be praying for you, too."

He kissed her forehead. "God be with you, Anna."

"And with you, Levi."

He picked up his bundle. "Keep Ellie in here until I get out of sight, so she won't get upset." He walked out quickly, wanting to get away before he couldn't force himself to leave.

Keeping the sun at his back, Levi traveled west, hoping he'd come to something he recognized. He stopped for lunch and ate the ham biscuits Anna had packed him. His heart felt crushed from leaving her, but she gave him no other option. He felt like crying, but he refused to give in to tears for fear they wouldn't stop.

He got up to continue on when he noticed something white in the distance. He went to investigate and found a corpse or what was left of it. The man had been dead for a while, and the wild animals had picked the bones pretty clean.

He felt around the pockets of the clothing left and found a few coins, a knife, and a pocket watch. On the back of the case were engraved the initials, "H.R." It had to be Hiram Ramsey, Anna's father-in-law. Since his rifle lay nearby and his pockets hadn't been stripped, Levi assumed he'd been killed in an accident or by a wild animal.

He didn't have a shovel, but he put the body in a trench of sorts and covered it with rocks. He quoted the Twenty-Third Psalm and said a prayer. Maybe this would be a reason to pay Anna a visit later on and let her know.

Levi walked and walked. He'd almost given up on finding anything familiar, when he began to recognize the terrain. He came up to the spot with his rock, and he knew where he was.

Daylight had faded fast, so he decided to stop and build a fire before it got any darker. He'd be at Noah's in time for breakfast tomorrow.

Anna had given him a blanket in which to carry his things in case he needed to spend the night, and he made his bed from it. He'd just stretched out when he heard the cry of a mountain lion in the distance. Maybe he should have tried to make it to Noah's cabin, even in the dark. He sat up and threw another piece of wood on the fire.

Levi startled awake with the feeling of being watched. He reached for his gun and looked around but could see nothing out of the ordinary.

He made sure the fire was out and gathered his things. When he got to the farm, Noah had just come from the barn carrying the milk buckets. He dropped the buckets the moment he saw Levi and came running, hugging him tightly.

"We were afraid something had happened to you. Where have you been?"

"Something did happen, but I survived. Come on, I'll tell you over breakfast, and I'm starved."

Violet gave a little scream when she saw him, ran over, and threw her arms around him.

He stiffened. "Isn't that being a bit improper, Miss Dixon?"

She gasped and stepped back. "I-I...We thought you were dead."

"Well, as you see, I'm not." Levi hated being abrupt, maybe even rude, but he had no intention of putting up with her antics this time.

Daisy set breakfast on the table, and they began to fill their plates. "Now tell me what happened," Noah demanded.

Levi told them of the blizzard and him cutting his leg. He told of making his way to a cabin after he saw the light from the window. "A widow and her daughter took care of me. I developed a fever and infection, and was unconscious for several days. Even after I started to heal, the weather remained too bad to travel out."

"How old was the daughter?" Violet asked.

"Not nearly as old as me." He didn't want to divulge too much information about Anna, because he wanted to protect her reputation.

"Where was their cabin?"

"I'm still not sure. I found it by accident and didn't know how I'd gotten there. I came west to get back here, so it must be to the east."

Noah looked at him quizzically, but didn't say anything. He knew Levi usually had a good sense of direction. "Well I'm glad you're back, and you came just in time for spring planting."

Anna came from the barn and looked in the direction Levi had left three days ago. Never had she imagined she would miss the man this much. In some ways, he'd become family.

She heard Ellie and hurried to the house. She'd left the child asleep in the bed and hoped she'd stay there until Anna returned.

Ellie was sitting up in the bed crying when Anna went to the bedroom. "Da-da. Da-da." She had been crying for Levi on and off for three days.

"Levi had to go to his home."

"No-o." Ellie shook her head vigorously. "Want Da-da."

Truth be told, Anna wanted Levi, too. She shook her head, too. No, this was for the best. With a little more time, they'd get over him.

She split some left-over biscuits and heated the halves in butter in a frying pan. They'd eat these and some cherry preserves for breakfast. She didn't cook as often now that Levi was no longer here.

Ellie ate some, drank her milk, and played for a while. Then, she started fussing for "Da-da" again. Anna picked her up and cuddled her to her. As Ellie cried herself to sleep, Anna felt silent tears slip down her own face.

By July, Ellie only cried for Levi now and then, and pain didn't stab Anna as hard. She had given Ellie a spoon and set her at the edge of the garden to dig in the dirt while Anna hoed in the cool of the evening. The garden looked as good as when Elbert and Mr. Ramsey had planted it.

"Da-da! Da-da!" Ellie got up and started running as fast as her little legs would take her. Anna looked and saw Levi striding toward them. Her heart nearly jumped from her chest at the sight of him.

He scooped up Ellie and hugged her tightly, still watching Anna. Anna walked toward him, wanting to run and feel his arms wrap around her but making herself walk slowly. "What are you doing here?" It came out sharp, but perhaps that would disguise how glad she was to see him and how good she thought he looked.

He'd shaved off his beard, and his handsome face almost took her breath. Why did God have to make the man so good-looking?

His smile faded with her harsh question. "I came to give you news. Let's go inside for a minute." He shifted Ellie to one arm and put his hand on Anna's back. His touch sent tingles radiating out.

"I found a body on my way home. These things were in his pocket." He placed the objects on the table. "With the initials on the watch, I think it might be Mr. Ramsey."

Anna looked at the items and nodded. "Those are his. Could you tell what happened?"

"I'm guessing a bear or mountain lion got him, but there wasn't enough left to tell. He'd been dead for some time from the looks of things."

Anna felt weak. She didn't know if Mr. Ramsey would have wanted her and Ellie to stay without Elbert, but she didn't want anything like this to happen to him. "He told me the place would be mine if something happened to him. I wonder if he had a premonition he wouldn't return. D-do you think it's the same mountain lion that killed Elbert?"

"Hard to say, but it's possible. In fact, I've heard the cry of one myself a few times. Anna, what's wrong?" He leaned over and put a hand over hers. "You look so pale."

She didn't answer him. How could she tell him how the thoughts of him facing a killer mountain lion made her feel? "How far away is your brother's place?"

"A good day's walk and maybe a bit more. I spent the night outside when I returned and arrived around breakfast time, and I left this morning before sunrise. I brought a lantern this time."

"Oh, I should have sent one with you when you left."

"That's okay. I didn't think of it either."

She looked outside and saw the sun setting. "You'll stay the night? I hate to think of the dangers of returning in the dark."

His face relaxed, and the tension in his shoulders seemed to ease. "I had hoped you'd ask, but I brought the lantern and a blanket in case."

Had she been so cold with him he didn't know if she'd even show common hospitality? She knew she could trust him. The issues, however, were her reputation and her resolve.

"Did you tell your family about me?"

His eyes twinkled. "Only that a widow and her daughter took care of me. They've tried to pick me for more information, but I've been intentionally vague."

That he would try to protect her this way pulled at her heart strings. "Let me fix us some supper. I haven't started anything. How does some breakfast for supper sound? I could fry some meat, cook some eggs, bake biscuits, and make some grits."

"That sounds good. I've missed your cooking."

He sounded sincere, and the comment made her happier than it should have. She'd always found Levi an easy man to please, but at least he told her.

Ellie wouldn't let Levi put her down, and so he held her. She seemed content just to sit on his lap and put her head against his chest.

"You shaved your beard."

Levi smiled. "I did. I normally shave it for the summer and grow it back in the fall. Do you like me better with the beard or without?"

She didn't want to tell him what seeing him without the beard did to her. "I like you either way." Oh, my! That didn't sound any better. She shouldn't have said it either.

Levi's smile turned into an all-out grin, but he didn't make some flirty remark as she feared he would. "I also found Mr. Ramsey's rifle, but I didn't bring it today, since I carried mine. I can come back sometime on horseback and bring you his if you want. I cleaned it good from where it lay out in the elements."

She bit her lip before she answered. Her mind wanted her to say one thing, and her heart wanted her to say another. She went with her mind. "No, don't come back. I had…. Ellie had just begun to get over you, and look at her now."

She nodded at her daughter. The little girl had snuggled into him and gone to sleep.

Levi gave her such a disappointed look, she almost changed her mind. He looked down at Ellie and then up at Anna, and she could read the expression on his face as plain as if he'd said it. "At least she's glad to see me."

"Are you sure? You could sell it if you didn't want to keep it."

It took her a second to realize he referred to the rifle. "I'm sure. Elbert's gun is all I need, and you did find Mr. Ramsey. Sell it if you want." She'd rather not have the money the gun would bring than to have Levi visit like this again. Now they'd have to get over him all over again.

Chapter Twelve: Visits

Levi carried Ellie to the bedroom and helped tuck her in. Anna's wayward heart sent images of him crawling in that bed beside of Anna and her waking up snuggled against him. She couldn't believe she stood there pining for another man.

She turned and headed for the chair beside the fireplace. He followed and pulled another close where he'd sat so many times before.

"I wouldn't know your leg had been injured your limp is so slight now," she told him. "Does it bother you any?"

"A little if it turns cool or rainy, but it's healed nicely. You did a good job."

She'd forgotten how easily compliments and appreciation rolled from his lips. She'd missed hearing a kind word.

"Shall we have our Bible reading?"

Anna reached for the Bible and handed it to him. She'd missed having their devotion together, too.

"Have you seen any more of the Hickses?" he asked after they'd finished reading and praying.

"No, and I'm praying it stays that way."

His eyes softened. "I am, too. I'm praying for you and Ellie every day, for your well-being."

She told him about Ellie's progress, how she'd begun to talk more and could now run around, and related some of the toddler's antics. They laughed together over some of the child's escapades.

"I miss her so much." Levi sounded so sincere she couldn't doubt him. "And I've missed you, too." His sapphire-blue eyes pierced her to the heart.

She looked away. She wouldn't tell him how much she'd missed him, although she gritted her teeth to keep the words from sliding off her tongue. "We should be going to bed," she said instead. They had already stayed up late talking. She suddenly realized how her statement could be misconstrued, but Levi didn't appear to take it wrong.

He nodded. "I'll need to leave in the morning for the long trip." His eyes begged her to tell him not to go, but she couldn't. No matter how warm and caring Levi seemed, she would not marry a man she didn't love – never again.

Anna woke up the next morning with sunlight streaming through the small bedroom window. How late had she slept?

She looked over at Ellie, and the child had vanished! She panicked until she remembered Levi. Surely he would have Ellie.

She hurriedly jerked on her dress and slipped on her socks and shoes, not even bothering to comb her hair. They sat in the floor playing with some scraps of wood Levi must have brought in from the barn.

He smiled up at her. "I hope you rested well."

She did. She'd slept much sounder than when he wasn't here. "You should have awakened me. I need to hurry and milk."

"I took care of milking and the outside chores. I even strained the milk for you, covered the crock, and put it in the springhouse. When I heard Ellie awake, I went and got her so you could sleep longer."

She mumbled her thank-you, embarrassed by being such a sluggard this morning. "I'll get us some breakfast, then."

He had already made coffee, and she helped herself to a cup to sip as she prepared them something to eat. A part of her wished that she needed to put something on to cook a big dinner for Levi, but she tried to divert her thinking. However, his presence filled the cabin, and she couldn't get her thoughts to settle on anything else for long.

They lingered at the table after they'd finished eating with Levi seeming to hate to leave as much as she wished he didn't have to. "You need to be going," she finally told him. "I hate to think of you spending the night outside, and it's too late now for you to make it in one day."

His eyes showed his hurt before he looked away. "Then there's no need to rush, is there?"

"I certainly don't want you having to spend two nights camping out."

"It'll be all right. The weather is warm now, and I've spent many a night out hunting when the weather wouldn't be nearly this pleasant."

"Have you heard the mountain lion again?"

The hurt went from his face. Had asking about the beast showed him she cared? She didn't want him to get the wrong idea.

"Not recently." He drank the last of his coffee and stood.

When he went to hand Ellie to Anna, the child screamed. "No! No-o-o! Want Da-da." Big tears ran down her cheeks.

"Here." Levi put out his hands to take her again. "I'll walk around outside for a bit to settle her down."

Anna stood at the window and watched Levi carry Ellie slowly around the backyard, pointing to objects and talking to her. She had a long list of tasks she needed to be about, but she didn't want to turn from Levi when he'd be leaving shortly. The man had become her best friend – her only friend really. But now, as single woman, it wouldn't be right to let him stay for any longer than necessary.

Levi sat Ellie down on the ground, let her run around, and played with her. Anna could hear her daughter's cackles from inside the cabin. When Ellie grew tired, Levi picked her up and brought her inside. He held her until she fell asleep, which didn't take long.

After he carried Ellie to the bedroom, Anna helped him put her down for her morning nap. They tiptoed out, and Levi turned to her. "Walk out with me?"

She nodded, afraid she couldn't talk around the lump growing in her throat. They walked out together.

"I care a great deal about you, Anna. I wish you'd consider letting me court you."

"Courting usually leads to marriage."

"I know." He looked at her intently, trying to determine how she felt.

She looked away. "I can't. I can't marry again."

He reached out and took her hand. She wanted to jerk it back, but she couldn't bring herself to do so. Something about Levi gave her strength and support, and she needed that right now.

"I understand if you need more time. Just promise me that you'll consider my offer. Don't go marrying one of the Hickses or something."

She knew he wanted to lighten the mood and move past her rejection, and she appreciated him being so considerate, despite her refusal to court him. She smiled a weak smile.

"It's all right, Anna." He pulled her into a gentle hug, and she felt cherished. "May God bless and protect you." He kissed the top of her head, turned abruptly, and walked away with a quick stride without looking back.

Anna didn't make it inside the cabin before the tears came, but she held the sobs until she'd shut and barred the backdoor. Then she cried her heart out.

Levi forced himself to walk away from Anna quickly, and he didn't dare look back. Maybe she'd been right, and he shouldn't have come. Leaving seemed even harder this time than before.

He'd hoped she'd missed him enough that she would welcome him back with open arms. He'd dreamed that she would tell him how much she loved him and they could marry before another winter. He should have known better.

He looked up, seeing only a bit of sky beyond the canopy of the forest. "Lord, what am I to do now?"

Love her. Court her. Did those words come from God or from his own mind? How could he court her when she didn't want to see him?

He could have sworn there'd been moments when he saw tenderness in her eyes. At least she seemed to like him, but how much did she care for him, and would he ever get the chance to know?

Love her. He already did that. She had stolen his heart long before he'd left the first time, although she must not have wanted it at all.

Court her. Could he court her without seeing her? The distance made it hard but not impossible. An idea began to form in his mind, and he grinned as he considered the plan.

Ellie woke up and looked for Levi. She couldn't understand what had happened to him or where he'd gone. She cried and called "Da-da," and Anna felt like crying with her.

That night Anna sat before the cold fireplace and tried to comfort her daughter. Levi should have to watch what a problem he'd caused by his impromptu visit.

Ellie finally cried herself to sleep, and Anna put her to bed. Feeling restless, she went back to her lonely chair before the hearth, and picked up her Bible. It fell open to a passage in Ruth, "Intreat me not to leave thee, or to return from following after thee: for whither thou goest, I will go; and where thou lodgest, I will lodge...." She slammed the Book closed.

Just then she heard the cry of a mountain lion in the distance, and it sent chills down her spine. "Lord, please keep Levi safe. Protect him through the night and see him home without mishap, I pray."

Gradually, Ellie's fussy spells became less frequent, and Anna stayed busy trying to harvest and preserve what she could from the garden. The woodpile worried her the most. She had gathered small fallen logs and larger branches from the forest, but she hesitated to venture too far since she'd heard the mountain lion. She managed to saw the larger ones into lengths that would fit into the fireplace, but the awkwardness of the task showed her she had little skill with sawing. On the last, she gathered some smaller pieces, thinking they would be better than nothing. Still, she feared she didn't have nearly enough to see them through the winter, especially if it turned out to be as rough as the last one. She estimated she had about half the amount Elbert and Mr. Ramsey usually gathered.

September days brought a chill in the air, and some mornings frost clung to the ground when she went out to milk. She needed to go into Boone to buy supplies and staples for the winter, but she procrastinated. For some reason, she hesitated to leave her cabin sanctuary. At one time, she'd have been thrilled at the prospect of shopping, but now it made her feel susceptible. Had she become a recluse?

She went out to milk as always, hurrying to get her outside chores completed before Ellie awoke. She milked the cow, fed and watered the animals, and gathered the eggs. On her way back to the cabin, she glanced at the woodpile. It had doubled in size! She blinked, not believing what she saw.

She stopped in front of the pile to examine it more carefully. She could tell the neatly cut and stacked new wood from her poor attempts. Some of it had even been split, something she had not done on any of the ones she'd gathered.

Who would have done this? The Hicks brothers? Levi? The Hickses didn't seem to have the disposition to help someone unless they thought they would gain from it. But perhaps they thought this would make her more agreeable to marrying one of them. Levi had the heart for helping, but he lived so far away. She couldn't fathom how he'd manage to carry so much wood all this distance.

Well, she should be thankful someone had, for it took one worry from her. *Thank Thee, Lord, because I know this must have been Thy orchestration .*

She went to the smokehouse in October to get the last of the bacon to fix. She would have to set plenty of rabbit gums to have some meat. She planned to also kill a few chickens along, but she needed to keep most of the hens for their eggs.

When she opened the door and saw meat hanging from the rafters, the surprise didn't hit her as hard as the woodpile had. Not only had someone hung cured venison, but she saw bacon, side meat, and a ham. This would be more than she and Ellie would use through the winter.

However, despite the generosity of her Good Samaritan, the thought that someone could sneak about without her knowing it didn't set well. She clutched her rifle tighter in her hand.

In the middle of October, Anna got herself and Ellie ready, hitched up the wagon, drove around to the front of the cabin, and started down the mountain. She hoped she could stay on the unmarked trail and make it to Boone in a timely fashion.

To begin with, it looked like someone might have been this way since Mr. Ramsey and Elbert, but that soon changed, and going proved slow. She had to pick her way between the trees, and at times, she just prayed that she had taken the right path. When she saw the road leading to Boone, then the trees thin out, and finally a glimpse of the town in the distance, she breathed a sigh of relief.

Ellie had napped on the last of their trip. Anna woke her and headed for the store, the largest building she saw. As soon as she opened the door and walked in Ellie yelled "Da-da!" and began leaning forward with her arms outstretched. She looked up to see Levi there with an attractive woman with flaming red hair. The woman had her hand on Levi's arm.

"Anna!" He looked stunned but gathered himself and came to them, taking Ellie. *Lord, why this? Now I'll have to wean Ellie from him again.*

The young woman came to stand with him. "Who is this?" She looked unhappy. "And why is this child calling you 'Daddy?' Re-a-l-ly, Levi?"

Chapter Thirteen: Trouble

Levi took a deep breath, as if he didn't like the situation either. "Anna, allow me to introduce my sister-in-law's sister, Violet Dixon. Miss Dixon, this is Anna Ramsey and her daughter, Ellie." He ignored Violet's other question.

The young woman looked at Levi. "Why aren't you calling me 'Violet'? Are you calling me 'Miss Dixon' for her benefit?" Then she turned to Anna. "Where is your husband, Mrs. Ramsey?"

"I'm calling you 'Miss Dixon,' because that's all I ever call you, especially after I came back."

Anna looked at Levi, still trying to decide what all this meant. Was Levi courting this woman? Why else would they be together here without a chaperone? But that would certainly be improper.

"Her husband is dead." Levi answered for her.

"This is not the widow you stayed with is it?" Violet's voice screeched.

Levi hesitated. "That is none of your business, now is it?"

Violet huffed. "Well, I guess you just answered my question. I'm surprised at you, Levi. I thought you had higher moral standards than to dally with some woman."

Levi's eyes became dangerously dark. "We did not dally. Anna diligently nursed me back to health. I would have been dead but for her help."

"What's all this? Violet, everybody in the store can hear you." The woman looked a little like Violet, except more subdued and less flashy.

"Anna, allow me to introduce you to my sister-in-law, Daisy. Daisy, this is Anna Ramsey and her daughter, Ellie."

"The widow who Levi stayed with all those months," Violet added.

"What a pretty little girl." Daisy smiled at Ellie, and then looked back to Anna. "My husband will hate he missed meeting you. He pulled a muscle in his shoulder, and stayed home with our daughter, Iris. She looks to be a little older than Ellie."

"Ellie called Levi 'Daddy.'" Violet gave Anna a withering look.

As if to prove the woman's point, Ellie reached up, rubbed Levi's cheek, and said "Daddy," much clearer than ever before.

"My husband died not too long after Ellie was born. She came to like Levi, and 'Da-da' became easier for her to say," Anna explained.

"You shouldn't have to explain anything to them."
Levi's face looked like granite.

"With her light coloring, the child doesn't look
anything like Levi," Daisy said. "And besides, we know
how devout he is in his faith." She gave her sister a
cutting look. "Haven't you often lamented you wish
he'd flirt some with you?"

"Fine. Take his and her side over your own
sister's." Violet stomped off.

Daisy looked at Anna. "I apologize, Mrs. Ramsey.
Violet has always been rather high-strung and
immature."

"Amen to that," Levi mumbled, not looking at all
happy about what had transpired.

"I must be about my shopping and get home."
Anna reached to take Ellie, but she buried her face in
Levi's shoulder.

"Let me hold her for you while you shop."

Knowing that it would be faster that way and
would prevent Ellie from throwing a fit, Anna nodded.
The faster she bought the things she needed and got out
of here, the better.

Anna feared Levi might try to follow her, but he
didn't. He walked around with Ellie, talking to her and
naming object after object for her to say. She loved the
game.

Anna handed the clerk her list of stables to fill,
while she browsed for the few items she needed to
select. Ellie needed some warm dresses. She fingered a

pretty bolt of blue gingham, but she could make do with
what she had, and Ellie needed something warmer. The
wool plaids were pretty, but a smaller print or solid
would be better for Ellie. In the end she bought a yard
each of lilac, pink, and white flannel and some yellow
and green wool with smaller checks. She would use the
white for undergarments or a shift for Ellie.

When her purchases were loaded, Anna reached
for Ellie. Of course, she screamed at the top of her
lungs. Levi looked grief-stricken. "I hope you know I
have no feelings for Violet Dixon," he told her. "And
I'm sorry Ellie's so upset."

"It's this way for days, and sometimes weeks,
every time you leave her." She drove away with him
looking devastated.

All the way home, Anna fumed. As possessive as
Violet had been, there had to be more to her and Levi's
relationship than he wanted Anna to believe. She
shouldn't care. It shouldn't bother her, but it did.

And the nerve of the woman insinuating that Anna
was nothing more than a trollop. Even with all the
different personalities at the orphan house, Anna had
never met a more judgmental, rude woman. Why, she
appeared every bit as immature as Ellie. At least her
sister, Daisy, seemed to be reasonable.

Well, she could just view the incident as one more
reason she should stay as far away from Levi as
possible. Even if he were innocent as he wanted her to
believe, she didn't need a handsome man that women

flocked around like chickens to their feed. For that matter, she didn't need a man at all.

She carried her sleeping daughter into the house and put her to bed. After going back to the barn and unhitching the wagon, she did all the evening chores, using the lantern for the last of them. She only took the small items in the house. She'd unload the heavy sacks in the morning.

Although she crawled into bed exhausted, sleep didn't come for a long time. She couldn't dismiss thoughts of Levi or Violet as she wanted.

The next morning, Anna rose early, despite her restless sleep. She did the chores and unloaded some more of the wagon, but she couldn't pick up the larger bags. Finally, she got a tarp, helped the heavy sacks to fall to it without bursting, and dragged it to the house.

Before the weather turned really cold, Anna went out to do her morning chores and found bags of cornmeal sitting against the house. She looked at the corncrib to see most of the corn had been taken. Someone had exchanged the ears of corn for the meal, something she appreciated, since she didn't know where to take it to get it done. However well-intended, though, the secrecy of these visits made her uneasy.

The first real snowfall didn't come until the week before Christmas. Anna had made Ellie the yellow wool dress for Christmas, and she would finish wrapping a string ball from fabric scraps left from cutting all the new clothes. She'd made the flannel dresses first.

Christmas Day looked like it might be a pretty day. The temperature would likely warm to above freezing like yesterday, and the snow had melted, leaving the ground wet but not so slick.

Anna had slept later than usual, so she hurried to dress and get outside before Ellie awoke. She opened the back door to find a beautiful rocking chair with intricate carving. Beside it sat a smaller one with a frolicking rabbit on its top back. She sucked in her breath. Levi?

A note on the large chair seat confirmed it. "Every mother should have a rocking chair, and Ellie can rock her doll. Merry Christmas, Levi."

The thoughtful gesture brought tears to her eyes. But why had he done this? She could almost hear him say, "So you could have a Christmas present."

A bucket of milk sat beside the chairs. He had done her chores, too. How had he managed all this? Had he traveled all night? The thoughts of him out all night in the frigid temperatures worried her. Even if she didn't want to see him, she didn't want anything bad to happen to him.

But you do want to see him, her conscience nagged. She refused to listen. The sooner she purged Levi West from her thoughts the better. But how could she do that when he did things like this? And most likely, he had been responsible for the firewood and the meat, too.

Christmas turned out to be joyous. Ellie loved her presents, and Anna played with her for a long time. When it drew close to time for her nap, Anna rocked her to sleep in the new rocking chair. Oh, if she had only had this when Ellie was a baby.

She couldn't stop herself from wishing Levi were here to share the day with them like last year. The thought crossed her mind that her life would have been very different if she'd married Levi instead of Elbert. There was nothing cold or inconsiderate about Levi.

She found it hard to believe this was her third Christmas on the mountain. But how different they all had been! The first one with Elbert had been sparse with little celebration, except what she'd been able to do on her own. Last year's had been the best, and she could still remember the joy of it. Levi's presence had made it special. This one would be better now thanks to him, but there would still be a loneliness hanging over the day, and both she and Ellie would miss him. His accident had been both a blessing and a curse. Now she and Ellie missed what they wouldn't have before.

As Ellie's birthday neared, Anna wondered if Levi would come again to bring a present. The possibility seemed likely, so she decided to compose a letter to him. She started twice and set each one aside. This had to stop. She would use the back sides, but she didn't have paper to waste. Although she didn't feel satisfied with her third attempt, she decided to use it anyway.

Dear Levi,

I appreciate all your help. You've made this winter much more pleasant for Ellie and me. However, I must ask you to stop. I can't grow to rely on you like this, and you mustn't continue to bring me these gifts. You are bound to marry and start a family of your own soon, and no wife would want you to show another woman such attention. I will always consider you a friend, but you must become a friend of the past for both our sakes.

It also scares me that you make such a long trip in the winter weather. I would hate for you to have another mishap. Even in other seasons, you have to spend the night in the wilds, and that mountain lion and other wild beasts are still out there. I've heard it myself.

Again, thank you for your kind thoughtfulness. I will remember it and your stay with fondness.

Sincerely,

Anna

Perhaps she shouldn't have added that last line. Did it sound too caring? She didn't want to give him any hope that they might have a future together.

Levi headed for Anna's cabin, hoping the weather didn't turn as nasty as those clouds threatened. At least he didn't have to bring the wagon this time, so he could make the trip faster, especially since he'd decided to ride his horse. However, to get through the forest and the low hanging limbs, it might have been better to walk. But since he'd made the trip a couple of times now, he thought he could take a path that would be less overgrown.

When he'd had to bring the wagon for larger loads, like the firewood, he'd gone in the front way to have a path wide enough for the wagon. He'd waited until he knew Anna would be in bed and likely asleep and spent the night in the barn. Then he had to leave before sunup the next morning, although he could park the wagon out of sight and continue home in the daylight.

Even though Anna called the bedroom extension to the cabin the back bedroom, it had really been built to the far side. That meant that Anna wouldn't be as likely to hear anything.

He made it to the cabin just before nightfall and waited in the forest for a while. Since the horse made less noise than the wagon, he led it to the barn earlier than before. The wind had come up and made it colder than ever.

He huddled in an empty stall and threw some hay over him before covering it with his blanket. Although the insulation helped, he guessed he'd be in for an uncomfortable night, but at least he'd be away from the wind for the most part. It would be worth it to get Ellie's birthday present to her, and he'd included something for Anna, since he didn't know when her birthday would be.

He wished he could see her face in the morning. Maybe he could. Did he dare hide in the edge of the forest and watch from a distance. He might not be able to see the expression on her face, but he could see her.

He didn't like being so close to Anna and not being with her, but she'd made it clear she didn't want him coming around. Would she ever? Would her heart soften eventually? Even if his efforts never brought her affection, she needed help, and he intended to help her as much as he could.

He wondered for the hundredth time what her husband had been like and how he'd turned her from the idea of marriage. Anna never wanted to talk about it, although she'd hinted that their relationship hadn't been what she'd hoped for.

Had Anna believed that he had no interest in Violet? Those two women were worlds apart and the more he lived around Violet, the harder he found it to even like her. But at the store, Violet had tried to make it appear as if they were a couple, and he and Anna had wronged her by having an illicit affair. Sometimes he felt like throttling the spoiled, selfish woman.

He woke up chilled to the bone. How he'd like to be able to build a fire, or better yet, share Anna's.

He had to light the lantern to see by, but he expected Anna to still be sleeping soundly or at least in bed. First, he took his packages to the back porch but saw a note with "Levi" written on it tacked to a porch post.

He took it back to the barn and sat down to read it. The letter pretty much restated what she'd told him before. Although it didn't mention Violet at all, he could read between the lines when she said, "You are bound to marry and start a family of your own soon, and no wife would want you to show another woman such attention."

The fact that she worried about him making the trip brought a smile to his face. She did care about him, but was it truly just as a friend like she wanted to believe? She had asked him to quit bringing gifts. He would consider honoring her wishes, but material things were not the only way to help. Come spring, there would be other ways.

To prove his point, he milked, fed the animals, and gathered the eggs for her. She should be up before any of it froze on the back porch. He wished he had paper and pen to reply to her letter, but he probably didn't have time anyway.

He saddled his horse, collected his things, and slipped into the forest. Wrapping his blanket around himself, he sat down on a huge rock where he could see the back of the cabin if he peeped around the large tree in front of him. The wind had died down, and he should be well enough hidden from sight.

He didn't have to wait long. Anna came out and stopped short when she saw the things on the porch. She looked around, but didn't let her gaze stop on him. She gathered up the things and took them in the house, making two trips.

He wished he could have seen her open them, but at least he'd been able to see her. That image would have to see him through the rest of the winter. He didn't plan to return until spring.

Anna set the two packages wrapped in store paper and a wooden box on the table, and pulled the note out of the top of one.

Dear Anna,

I wanted to share in Ellie's birthday, even though you don't want me to visit. The box is for Ellie, as well as the package I've marked for her. I figured she's growing so fast she will need new clothes come spring and summer.

Since I don't know when your birthday is, I've included a package for you as well. Please accept it as part of my deep appreciation for all you've done for me. I have a fond regard for you that no amount of scolding can erase.

Did you ever think that God may have led me to your door that night for some other reason than just to save my worthless hide? Could He have a better, more glorious plan than we can imagine? Think about it, Anna. Pray about it. Be open to the possibility. In the meantime, please be careful and take care of yourself and Ellie. Know that you're always in my prayers. May God pour out His blessings upon you.

Affectionately yours,
Levi

Obstinate man! She reluctantly opened the package marked with her name to find three dress lengths of material – one a pale, sky blue of cotton so fine it resembled silk, the blue gingham she'd admired at the store in Boone, and a plaid of blue, red, and green. The extravagance of what he'd done made her take a seat. Did he think he could buy her affection?

She pushed the fabric aside and got up to strain the milk and put the eggs away. She wouldn't have to go to the barn in the cold this morning, but Levi would be traveling all day in it just so he could bring her and Ellie presents. That thought stayed with her until she finished the tasks. Then she sat back down at the table, put her head in her hands, and cried.

Ellie opened her package to find three pieces of material to make her spring dresses. Levi had made the box to hold wooden building blocks in different sizes he had shaped and sanded. Ellie loved them.

She played with Ellie for a while, and then left the girl to stack the blocks on her own while Anna sat and watched her. She picked up the yards of cloth and fingered the edges, enjoying the feel of it. Despite her displeasure that Levi had spent his money on her, a part of her appreciated his thoughtfulness. Would he always show this much concern for a woman he liked, even after he married her? How would she ever discern the true heart of any man?

Anna debated on whether or not she should tell Ellie they were from Levi, because she knew it would cause Ellie to want to see him; but in the end she did. Levi's work to get them here deserved at least that.

Anna said "Levi," but Ellie wanted "Daddy." Anna didn't think her daughter knew the full meaning of the word, but it had become her word for Levi. In a way, Levi was the closest thing to a father Ellie had ever known.

Chapter Fourteen: Planting

In April, Anna came out of the house to find the garden plowed and ready to plant. How had Levi managed this in the dark? There'd been a full moon, but had it been enough for him to see how to do all this, or had he also used a lantern?

She heard a rustling in the forest and picked up her rifle. She hoped it would be Levi, but she wouldn't chance it. Orin Hicks walked up, and she positioned the gun where she could easily raise it if needed.

He looked over the garden. "How'd you manage to git this done all by yourself?"

"I have my ways."

He looked over at the wood still stacked against the house. Levi had brought enough she hadn't had to use it all.

"I see you still have wood left over from the winter, too." He sounded disappointed. "I'd hoped you'd have had time to come to your senses."

"Mr. Hicks, I will never want to marry you. As you can see, I'm making it just fine without a husband."

"I shore wish you'd reconsider. Clem has found a woman to court over at Noah West's place, and I shore would like to have one, too."

She paused to reflect on what he said. He had to mean Violet. Who else would Clem be courting at Noah West's place? "Perhaps Violet has some sisters you could court. Why don't you have Clem ask her?"

He raised his eyebrows. "If they're anythang like Violet, I'll pass. That woman would drive a man crazy. I don't know how Clem puts up with her. If he marries her and brangs her home, I shore would like to have another place to move to." He looked around Anna's farm with approval. "How do you know Violet anyways?"

"I don't know her well, but we met at the store in Boone."

"I reckon that's likely enough fer you to know what I'm talkin' about."

Anna couldn't help but smile. She told herself her amusement came from the fact that not even Orin liked Violet and not from the fact that Violet's interests may have moved from Levi.

"You shore are purty when you smile. You orta smile more often."

The compliment surprised her. Had she misjudged the man? Did he have a softer side? She looked at his dirty, haggard appearance. Regardless, this would not be the man for her. They had little in common. If she ever did decide to marry again, she wanted someone who could carry on an educated conversation about the Bible, books, and things outside the mountain communities. Why did Levi's face suddenly appear in her mind?

"I reckon I'll better be goin' then. You thank on me and my offer now. All the work of runnin' a farm and the household can't be easy on you. I'd treat you and your daughter real good, and we'd have us some more youngins as well." With that he turned and left.

What a strange man. First he tries to force her to marry him and then he tries to cajole her. What would he do next?

Anna moved into the bed in the front room, the one Levi had used. She didn't know if he would come anytime soon or not, but she might hear him from here. She wanted to have a talk with him. The man had to stop this.

Ellie refused to make the move. "No. Big girl."

"I know you're a big girl, but don't you want to sleep in here with Mama?"

Ellie shook her head. "Daddy's bed."

"Well it's going to be Mama's bed now."

She let Ellie stay in the back bedroom to prevent the fuss, although Anna would miss her daughter being beside her at night. Maybe Ellie would change her mind.

On the night of the full moon in June, Anna awoke
to sounds outside. She dressed in the dim light filtering
in the window without lighting a lantern. She looked out
the window. A man worked in the back field. By his
stance and walk she felt sure it was Levi, but she took
her gun just in case.

"What are you doing here?"

Levi turned to face her. "I thought if you had this
planted in corn, you could sell or barter some of it if you
didn't need it all yourself."

"Why are you doing all this? It makes no sense.
Aren't you supposed to be helping on your brother's
place?"

"I work there, but I worry about you, Anna. You
deserve to have it easy, without worries." His voice
softened. "I care about you and Ellie. How's she doing?"

"Fine. Growing and getting stubborn."

"Like her mama." He chuckled.

"I am not stubborn."

He raised an eyebrow.

She looked away. Maybe she had been stubborn
with him. "Come into the house, I'll fix us some coffee,
and we'll talk."

He looked so natural sitting at his usual place at
the table. Maybe she should have thought before she
invited him in. "Are you going home in the morning?"
She glanced at the clock. "Or is it morning now?"

"Not yet, and it's up to you when I leave. I'm not
trying to force myself on you, but I want to make things

easier for you. I can stay if you need me. I'll sleep in the barn if that makes you more comfortable."

"Is that what you've been doing when you come?"

He hesitated and then nodded.

"It actually makes me feel better to know you've not been trying to travel in the dark, or you're not camping out through the night, but it must have been cold out there when you came at Christmas and for Ellie's birthday."

"I knew you didn't want me visiting you, so I tried to help without causing you distress."

"I just wanted to protect us…. I just wanted to protect Ellie from the constant partings. Thank you for the wonderful presents, by the way." Her eyes moved to the rocking chairs she and Ellie used daily.

"You're welcome. I knew you would see that Ellie had presents, but I wanted you to have some, too."

"They were very extravagant."

"No, they weren't. I would give you the world if I could. You already have my heart, my love, although you likely don't want that either."

"Y-y-you love me?"

"With all my being, with all my heart."

"What about Violet?"

"I never had any interest in Violet. It's kind of like you and the Hickses. Thankfully, she has another suitor now. Actually, it's Clem Hicks."

"I know. Orin paid me a visit and told me about it. I think he's hoping to move in here and let Clem have their place."

Levi turned pale. "And you agreed?"

"Absolutely not! Surely you know me better than that. I really don't want to marry anyone."

His face fell. "Are you telling me I don't stand a chance with you?"

"Would you quit doing all this work or bringing presents if I told you that you didn't?"

He shook his head. "My help isn't contingent on anything. It's given freely, because I want the best for you and Ellie. It's the same way with the presents. They're free gifts with no strings attached. But are you trying to avoid my question?"

"Maybe. To be honest, I don't know how I feel about you. I like having you around, but I'm not sure if it's friendship I feel or more."

"If you need more time, Anna, I'll understand and try to be patient. I'm not trying to pressure you. But would you tell me why you're so afraid of marrying again? I know you've hinted that your first marriage wasn't what you'd hoped for, but how did Elbert treat you, and what do you want from a husband?"

"I'm not sure it's wise to answer those questions."

"Why not? I'm already in love with you, and whatever you say isn't going to make me love you any less or love you more, but it will help me understand."

She took a deep breath. "Elbert didn't abuse me in any way, but he was never considerate either. He went about his business during the day and expected me to take care of my chores, do the housework, and have his meals ready. He never did anything to make my days easier or brighter, never even said a thank you or showed any appreciation. The only compliment he ever gave me was to say he liked my looks a couple of times. He never gave me a present, not even a wildflower. I will say, however, that Elbert didn't treat me as harsh as Mr. Ramsey did. My husband just normally treated Ellie and me as if we didn't exist and certainly weren't important, except for the times he turned to me at night. Even that was done quickly without any regard for my feelings."

She felt her face flush hot and hid it in her hands. Why had she added that last part? She couldn't believe she'd told Levi everything.

"Oh, Anna." Levi moved beside her, lifted her from her seat, and wrapped his arms around her. "You deserve so much more. I wish you would let me show you what it's like to be truly loved."

It felt so good to be comforted. Levi didn't judge her wayward tongue. He didn't even blame her for Elbert's coolness the way many people would have if they knew. But she shouldn't be here in his arms. She pulled away and wiped her eyes. "I'm sorry."

"Don't be." He wiped her tears for her with his thumbs. "I'm glad you told me. Now I know why you've tried to keep me at arm's-length, but surely you know I'm nothing like Elbert. Haven't I proved that to you?"

"Yes. You've been a considerate, caring friend. I couldn't ask for a better one."

"I'll accept that for now, but a friendship is a good basis for a successful marriage. Just remember I would love to be a kind, considerate, loving husband, but that will be up to you. If you need time, I'll give you time."

She nodded. "Thank you."

Ellie came patting into the room, wiping the sleep from her eyes. She stopped, stared a second, as if she didn't believe what she saw. "Daddy!" She came running into Levi's arms. He held her close. At least she had no reservations about loving him.

"And how is my little sweetheart this morning?"

She got down and went to her blocks. "Play."

He looked at Anna. "I can't believe how big she is or how well she's walking and talking."

"Well, she's two and a half now. It's a blessing to have her out of diapers, too."

Ellie looked up, put her hand on her chest, and said, "Big girl."

He laughed. "Yes, you certainly are a big girl, and a smart one, too."

She put out her hand and wiggled her fingers. "Come play."

Levi sat down on the floor with her and they started building with her blocks. "Do you like your blocks I made you?"

"Blocks." She held out one.

"I just hope she doesn't cry for days after you go this time." Anna sounded accusatory.

Ellie shook her head. "No. No go." She got up, came to Levi, and took his face between her little hands. "No go." She looked directly into his eyes.

"I have to go, Ellie, but not this minute. We can play for a while, but then I've got work to do before I go home."

"No go." Ellie started to cry.

"Here, here now. This won't do. Didn't you tell me you were a big girl? Big girls don't cry when they don't get their way. Look at Mama. She's not crying because I have to leave." If she did. Levi wouldn't go, but it would be wonderful if Anna cared that much.

Ellie looked at her mother and then back at Levi. "Play blocks."

"You're good with her," Anna said. "Play with her while I fix breakfast. After we eat, we'll all do the outside chores and then plant the field."

"That sounds like a good plan."

They worked all day together, only stopping for short breaks and for dinner, a stew that Anna had left simmering. By dusk, Levi felt tired, but satisfied they'd got the corn planted.

"I have some money Mr. Ramsey left," Anna told him at supper. "I'll need to go into town before winter for more supplies, but I hate going by myself."

"I'll be glad to come and take you."

"No, I didn't mean that. I just wanted you to know we aren't destitute."

"Let me come drive you to Boone, Anna. Please."

She searched his eyes. "That's asking too much. It's too far for you to come just to take me into Boone."

"No, it isn't. I'll spend the night in the barn, just like this time."

"Oh, all right. If you insist."

Her lips twitched, as if they wanted to turn up, but she didn't let them. He'd like to take the spunky, obstinate woman in his arms and kiss her senseless. He looked away.

"Ellie, it's your bedtime. Come on. Let's get you ready."

"No. Play wif Daddy."

Levi made his face show his disapproval. "Ellie. I know you didn't just tell your mother 'No.' My Ellie wouldn't do that."

Ellie hung her head, and he felt like scooping her up and kissing her, too, but he held his stern countenance. "Tell your mama you're sorry, and then go to bed like the good girl you are."

She looked up at Anna. "Sorrwe."

Anna gave him a grateful look, and took Ellie to the bedroom. After a while he heard Anna say, "Goodnight, darling. Sleep well."

"Night. Daddy."

"Do you want to tell Levi goodnight, too?" Anna came to the door. "She wants to tell you goodnight."

Levi went into the bedroom and kissed Ellie on the forehead. "Goodnight, sweetheart."

"Night, Daddy." Ellie patted the place beside her. "Daddy sleep wif Ellie."

"No, honey. I'm going to sleep in the barn."

"No, wif Ellie. Pl-ea-se, Daddy. Please sleep wif Ellie."

Levi didn't know what else to say. He looked at Anna.

She laughed. "Sometimes it was easier before she started letting her wishes be known."

"Levi and I are going to read the Bible before he goes to bed. I'll have him read it out loud, and you can lie here and listen to him."

"Daddy come here?" She patted the bed again.

"If Levi wants, he can sleep here when he's ready to go to bed."

He looked at Anna in surprise. He never thought she would allow him to spend the night in the house, much less in the bedroom.

"I've been sleeping in the other bed, so I might hear you when you came," Anna told him, "but Ellie has insisted on staying in here."

He looked back at Ellie. "You rest here, and I'll come to bed after a while."

She nodded. "Night, Daddy."

"Thank you," he whispered to Anna as they moved to the main room.

She shrugged. "You'll be more comfortable in here than out in the barn, and it made Ellie happy."

"You trust me?" He sat down in his usual chair after Anna seated herself in the rocking chair.

"I trust you." She sounded reluctant to admit it. "When you come again, please don't come in secret."

He couldn't help but smile that he'd made that much progress with her. Her trust had been hard won, and he knew he didn't have it completely for a long time.

"But you'll need to leave in the morning."

"I know." He'd made several giant steps forward this visit. She had moved into the front bed so she could know when he came in order to talk with him, she'd invited him into the cabin, she'd allowed him to spend the night in the bedroom, and the next time he came she wanted it to be a real visit with no sneaking around. The seeds of kindness he'd sown were beginning to sprout. He paused to thank God.

Chapter Fifteen: Courting

Something had changed in Anna, and she didn't understand it. Her days were better, brighter, as if a great burden had been lifted from her shoulders. But as far as she could see, nothing had changed.

After spending the night, Levi had left the following morning to go home. Her heart had cried to see him walk away, but this time he'd turned and waved before he disappeared into the forest. She liked Levi, and she doubted she would ever find a better friend.

Ellie had cried and fussed after him for a while, but Anna kept reassuring her daughter that Levi would come for another visit, and the girl had quieted sooner this time.

Anna stayed busy tending the garden and trying to keep the weeds from overtaking the cornfield, along with all her other chores. However, she still found herself looking forward to Levi's next visit. She should have allowed him to visit openly from the very beginning. Trying to keep him from making the trip certainly hadn't worked. And he'd called her stubborn!

She and Ellie stayed outside more during the summer months, and Anna had made them both bonnets to wear. But every uncommon noise she heard, ever crunch coming from the forest, she looked to the woods to see if Levi had finally come again.

When he came, however, he came in the front way driving a wagon filled with firewood. "I wanted to get an earlier start this year. I had to work hard last year to get enough here in secret for you to make it through the winter."

She didn't tell him she wondered if the good deeds might have come from the Hickses at first. She should have known better.

She propped on her hoe. "I'm about ready to call it a day, and it's about time for Ellie to get up from her nap. Come on in the house."

"I wondered where she'd gotten to. She usually runs to greet me."

"I told her that you'd be back to visit, and she's been looking for you."

He chuckled. "I had to force myself to wait a little while to return. I didn't want to seem too eager or wear out my welcome."

Anna laughed. "That would never happen, but it's good not to make it too often in case someone gets wind of it and thinks the worst."

He cocked his head at her. "I thought maybe I would come about once a month."

She knew he wanted her reaction. "That sounds about right, since the trip is so long."

"I'll just see to the horses first. You go on in, and I'll join you shortly. We can stack the wood after supper or even in the morning," He put out his hand. "Here let me take the hoe to the barn for you."

He turned and headed toward his team, so maybe he didn't notice she almost skipped into the cabin. Ellie would be so excited when she woke up.

"I don't have anything cooking." She tried to apologize as he walked up to the table. "I thought I would fry us some ham, bake some biscuits, and make some gravy to go with it."

"That sounds delicious."

She should have known Levi would be agreeable. On the other hand, if Elbert hadn't said anything about such a simple meal, Mr. Ramsey would surely have. "Let it go," she told herself. Best to leave the past in the past.

Ellie came into the kitchen, and a big grin spread across her face. She'd slept longer than usual and would likely want to stay up later tonight, especially since Levi had come. She ran to Levi and threw up her arms for him to seat her on his lap. They talked and played until Anna put supper on the table.

Levi looked across the table at Anna, and when she smiled at him, his heart did a flip. Something had changed in her, and he liked it. She seemed freer and not as reserved with him or as encumbered by her past. She even seemed happy and excited to see him, a miracle in itself. He'd begun to fear she would continue to push him away and never let him get close to her.

Since Anna now allowed him to visit with her and Ellie, it almost felt like he really courted her. Being here felt more and more like home. Truth be told, Anna and Ellie had become even more his family than Noah and Daisy, because his heart belonged here.

He played with Ellie while Anna did the dishes and straightened the kitchen, but he found himself watching Anna more than he should. She moved with such grace that the poem by Lord Byron, "She Walks in Beauty," came to mind.

He could see why Elbert would have chosen Anna to be his wife if he wanted a pretty woman. What he couldn't understand is why the man hadn't fallen madly in love with her. He could imagine her a few years ago, before a loveless marriage had changed her. She would have been young and innocent, looking to find someone to love her, since she didn't remember ever having that.

He turned his attention to Ellie. He couldn't believe Elbert hadn't been thrilled with his daughter, either. She was such a joy.

"I've started telling Ellie a Bible story each night and then she says a simple prayer before I blow out the light." Anna looked over at him as she took a seat on the floor to join them. "Maybe you can tell her the story tonight. I've been going through the Bible and choosing the stories suitable for a child her age. We're up to the one about Joshua and the wall of Jericho."

"That will be a good one." He smiled at the thought of animating and performing parts of the story to make it more interesting to Ellie. "I'll look forward to telling it to her."

When it became storytime, Levi watched with amusement as Anna's eyes widened and her lips turned into a smile over his illustrations of the men marching and blowing their horns. When the walls came tumbling down, Ellie jumped in surprise and then cackled in merriment.

Anna's smile became even broader. "You missed your calling as a stage performer, Levi."

He shook his head. "No, no. That's not my calling in life."

"And what is your calling?"

"First and foremost to be a godly husband and father. I like farming, but I could also be a furniture maker."

She blushed over the first part of his answer. Good. She'd gotten the message.

They put Ellie to bed. Her simple prayer moved Levi. "Tank you, God," she said with her eyes squeezed tightly shut. "Bwess Daddy and Mommy and me."

"Why do you think Ellie calls me 'Daddy'?" he asked Anna as they moved back into the living area. "I like it fine, but it seems odd because I know you didn't teach her to do it. One would think she'd have started calling me 'Levi' like she hears you do."

"I've pondered on that, too. My best guess is that I tried to teach her to say 'Daddy' for Elbert, and she must have transferred that to you. No matter how much effort I gave it, I could not get her to say 'Levi' instead."

They sat and talked and the time flew. Although the hour grew late, they made no effort to retire themselves. Levi wanted to spend every minute possible with Anna, and he knew from experience the time for him to leave would come all too soon.

The next morning began a wonderful day, full of hard work but also filled with fun and laughter. In fact, he'd never heard Anna laugh so much. He liked it; he liked it a lot.

Ellie had only taken a short nap that afternoon, and they planned to put her to bed earlier than the night before. The Bible story tonight had been about the prophetess, Deborah, so Anna told it.

"But I'm not nearly as good at this as you are," she protested.

"I just had an easier story," he told her. "I guarantee you I'll enjoy hearing yours even more than you liked mine."

She gave him a shy smile. She seemed to catch every nuance and hint he gave to compliment her. He would have liked to say more, because he knew she'd had so little of that in her life, but he didn't want to embarrass her or make her uncomfortable. They'd made great strides in their relationship, and he didn't want it to regress.

After they put Ellie to bed, he and Anna had their Bible reading and prayer – a good way to end the day. Now, if he could just take Anna to bed as his wife it would be even better. *Patience, Levi. Patience.*

Anna sighed after their devotion. "I'll hate to see you go tomorrow."

"Not as much as I hate to go." At least he'd gotten to spend two nights here this time. He should be thankful for his blessings.

Anna looked away still reticent of his hints that he wanted more. "Do you believe in long courtships, Levi?"

The question surprised him so much, he couldn't formulate an answer. What did she mean? Was she considering giving him permission to court her? Now, that would be progress by leaps and bounds.

"I guess that would depend on the situation. With the right woman, I would be glad for a courtship anyway I could get it."

"If you're agreeable to a long one with me, where I have the option of changing my mind, then I would be agreeable to you courting me."

His heart lurched, but his grin must have spread from ear to ear. He wouldn't dare indicate that he'd already been courting her, even without her permission. "Why did you change your mind?"

"I hesitate to say, lest you think ill of me."

"I would never think badly of you, Anna. Surely you realize that. I want us to be completely honest with each other and hold nothing back, no matter what. We need to trust the other will understand."

She blinked. "You once asked me what I wanted in a husband, and I didn't exactly answer you. You've just given the answer. I want an honest husband that shares everything with me, as I do with him. I want to love and be loved without reservations. I want to become one with a man, the way the Bible speaks of marriage."

How he wanted to be that man. "Does the permission to court you mean that you'll give me a chance to be that man?"

"Isn't that what courting usually means? And in many ways, you are the type of man I would choose, but please go slowly. I'm still so unsure that this is the right decision for me."

"We'll go as slowly or as fast as you want, but you never did tell me why you changed your mind about allowing me to court you." Her blush made his heart beat faster.

"You are an attractive man, Levi. Violet's attention may have turned to another, but I have no doubt that you would still rank above Clem Hicks if you wanted her back." Anna put up her hand to still his protest. "Not only are you handsome, but you're kind, considerate, and an overall good person. Even without Violet in the picture, you're bound to draw the interest of other women." Her face became a darker pink. "I'd like them to know you're taken."

He could scarce take in all she'd said. She thought him handsome and liked his personality. She might even be jealous of him, and she wanted others to know she had a claim on him. *Lord, if this gets any better, my heart will surely burst.*

"I guess it's better if I leave before Ellie awakes," Levi told Anna as they did the morning chores together at her insistence. He liked that she chose to spend as much time with him as possible.

"It is unless you want to see a stream of female tears." Did she mean she'd be crying for him, too?

"I'd much rather see her face light up with delight the way it does when she first sees me upon my return, and I'd prefer to hear her laughter."

Anna gave a half-grin. "Then you'll have to hurry back, won't you?"

He wanted to tell her if she married him, he wouldn't have to leave at all, but he wouldn't jeopardize this new-found rapport between them, and he'd promised her to take things slowly, at her pace.

When the time came, he hitched the wagon with Anna watching. He turned to her and took her in his arms. "Since I'm officially courting you, I'd like to give you a real kiss."

She gave a nervous laugh. "If we become engaged, it would be all right, but for now you'd better not. If you did, I might have a hard time moving as slowly as I need to, and I do want to be sure."

Her reasoning almost made him want to kiss her more, because his heart didn't desire to take things slowly. However, he needed to put her needs above his own, and she did need to be sure. If he disappointed her, if she found him lacking after marriage, it would be too painful to bear.

He kissed her low on her cheek instead and let his lips linger. Did she feel any of the sensuous feelings that washed through him? Maybe, for she leaned in as if she needed his support to stand.

"I'll be back before you know it," he whispered. A vast exaggeration he knew, but he said it for his benefit as much as hers. "Stay safe."

"You too." Her voice quivered, and he drove off quickly before he couldn't make himself go at all.

"Don't you think you're spending way too much time going back and forth to the widow's house?" Noah asked when he got back. Noah had been the only one he told where he went.

"Yes, I do. I'd like to marry the woman and never leave." Levi knew that wasn't what Noah meant, but he wanted his brother to know his intentions. "She's finally given me permission to court her."

Noah raised an eyebrow. "I thought that's what you'd been doing. Isn't that why you've been taking her firewood and such?"

Levi smiled. "It is, but now it's with her approval. At first I had to sneak around to help her out. I've found she has a stubborn streak."

"A stubborn wife could be a problem."

"Not this one, and she had her reasons. She had a cold first husband, and it's made her cautious, but she's coming around and beginning to warm to me."

Noah shook his head. "Well, I wish you the best, brother. Although I hate to see you move away from here, I knew it would come sometime. I've been lucky to have your help this long, considering how the women have always chased after you, but I'll miss you when you go."

"I'm not sure how soon that will be. Anna has made me agree to a slow courtship."

Violet cornered him alone in the barn during the evening milking time. "I want to give you one last chance to reconsider what we could have together. Clem is coming tomorrow, and I can tell him I've changed my mind about letting him court me."

"I'm courting another." How good it felt to be able to say that.

"The widow!" She didn't say it like a question.

He nodded. "I find myself drawn to her."

"I knew you two were closer than you indicated at the store in Boone."

"You're wrong. Anna didn't want me around her at that point. I've had to woo her cautiously, but she's finally becoming more receptive."

Violet gave a most unladylike snort. "I just bet she is." Innuendoes laced the retort. "I guess that's where you've been sneaking off to when you disappeared overnight." Her eyebrows shot up, and Levi's aggravation grew.

"I'll not have you insinuating Anna is anything but a moral, upstanding woman." Much more so than the woman standing before him, but he didn't add that.

"Well, when you regret your decision, it will be too late. Clem lives so far away that he doesn't get to come often, and I expect he'll ask me to marry him soon."

"I hope you two will be very happy together." He could say that in complete honesty. The farther Violet moved away from him the better.

Chapter Sixteen: Takeover

Anna had just put some venison on to cook and started out to hoe the garden when she saw Orin ride in, and he didn't have a friendly look on his face. She pushed Ellie behind her and pulled the door closed. She trusted Ellie to not get into anything. In fact, she'd probably stand right there by the door.

Orin not only rode his horse, he led a pack mule, too. He held his rifle across the front of his saddle. "Ann... er, Mrs. Ramsey. I'm tarred of waitin' on your decision. Clem's done asked that chatterbox to marry him, and she agreed. I'll give you two choices. Either agree to marry me or pack yourn and the girl's thangs and leave."

Anna gripped her rifle and started to raise it, but he had his up faster. "Don't you even thank about it."

"I haven't taken any time to make my decision." Anna tried to stare him down, despite the trembling she felt inside her. "I've told you 'no' from the very beginning."

"Then git your thangs, jist your personal items, mind you, and leave."

"T-this is stealing, and where am I supposed to go?"

"You marry me and you won't have that problem. I hear tell you're letting Noah West's brother come 'round courtin' you. If he's so much better than me, run to him."

Maybe Anna would. Could she find the West place? "Would you be so kind as to hitch up the wagon for me, while I pack our things?"

"Now, you don't need to be takin' no wagon. You won't be hauling that much. You and the girl can ride a horse. I'll let you tie your thangs on the second horse, but that's all you're taking. I'll need the rest for myself, since I'm leavin' most everythang for Clem."

Could she get in the house, bar the door, and shoot through the window? She certainly didn't want to endanger Ellie, but she didn't want Orin just to take everything they had either.

"You wait up a minute." He slid off his horse with his rifle. "I don't trust you in there. I'll just come along and watch you."

Picking up Ellie as soon as she walked into the cabin, she carried her to the bedroom. She took several pillowcases and packed up their things. She almost cried when she realized she couldn't take the rocking chairs. Maybe Levi would think of a way to help get their place back.

She went to the trunk and tried to hide what she packed by her body. She'd folded the money bag in a shirt, and she took it out quickly and stuffed it into her pillowcase.

She tied the stuffed pillowcases onto the horse and then saddled another one. Orin didn't want to set his rifle down to help. However, he did hand Ellie to her, once she'd led the horse to the chopping block and used it to climb into the saddle herself.

As Anna entered the forest and turned west, she remembered Levi saying he had trimmed a trail so he could ride a horse to her farm. She hoped she would be able to follow it. She guessed her situation could have been worse. At least Orin hadn't threatened to harm her or Ellie in any way.

She wished she'd thought to grab them something to eat, but she hadn't. When Ellie started complaining of being thirsty, Anna waited until they came to a place beside the creek that had a rock large enough she could use to get back in the saddle. It felt good to be off the horse.

After their break, Anna lifted Ellie up first and then managed to mount herself. They came to what looked to be another path intersecting with the one she'd traveled. It appeared less traveled and went more to the northeast. She wondered where it went, but continued west, wishing she had some idea how much farther it would be. She hadn't had much trouble following the trees Levi had trimmed.

She heard another horse coming up the path. Would that be Levi? Should she get off the trail and hide in case it wasn't? She didn't have time for a decision before the rider appeared. Clem. Her empty stomach lurched. And he had spotted her.

He pulled his horse up. "Whatcha doin' here?"

Didn't he know? "Orin ran me off my place. He told me I could either marry him or leave, and he pulled his gun on me."

Clem turned pale. Maybe he didn't know. "I'd best go try to talk some sense into him. The Wests ain't goin' to like Violet marryin' into the Hicks family if'n Orin's gonna act like this, and we've already set the date for the weddin' for Sunday after next. You go on to the West farm, and I'll head to your place."

"How far is it to Noah's farm?"

"Just a couple of hours or so."

Anna didn't know how long she'd ridden, but Ellie had gone to sleep in the saddle, and Anna had grown so weary and cramped of holding her that she had to take a break. She saw a large rock up ahead, and she hoped she could use it to mount easily again, but it looked precariously close to a drop-off. Still, she had to get out of the saddle for a few minutes and stretch.

She woke Ellie and had her hang onto the saddle horn while Anna dismounted. Then she reached up and helped Ellie down.

They climbed the rock and looked at the
spectacular view. Anna had never seen anything like it.

An ugly snarl drew her attention, and a huge
mountain lion crouched ready to spring. Anna knew
better than to try to run, but she eased down from the
rock, keeping Ellie behind her. Ellie must have sensed
her fear, because she remained quiet and did exactly
what Anna told her.

Staring into the beast's golden eyes, Anna
wondered if this was the one that had killed Elbert and
perhaps Mr. Ramsey. Would it kill her, too?

The cat slinked closer, and Anna could tell it was
ready to strike, when a shot rang out, and the mountain
lion fell. She looked up to see Levi hurrying toward her.

"Are you okay?"

"We are now." Anna leaned into his arms, letting
his strength encompassed her, because all of hers had
vanished.

Levi led her and Ellie to the rock and helped them
sit. Anna didn't know who clung to his hand harder, her
or Ellie. Levi sat down beside them. "Why were you this
far from your cabin? Has something happened?"

She told him what Orin had done, and his face
grew furious. "We'll see about this." But his face
softened when he looked at her.

"Why are you out here?" Anna knew it was too
early to be hunting.

"I often come out here." He looked out at the
scenery. "I call this my rock, and I tell it all my

problems. I talk to God here, and I can hear Him clearer. But come." He rose to help her up. "Let's get you to the cabin. I know you must be exhausted. Have you even had anything to eat?"

Anna shook her head. "Is it far to your cabin?"

"Not far at all."

"That mountain lion was mean." Ellie moved closer to Levi.

"I know, but he won't bother anyone again." Levi glanced over at the dead animal.

Levi helped Anna mount. This time Ellie rode with Levi, which helped keep Anna from cramping again.

Noah came out to meet them when they got to the cabin, and Levi introduced them. Noah led them into the cabin. Levi explained Anna's situation. "I'll get my rifle and two lanterns," Noah said.

"Anna told us Clem has gone to talk some sense into Orin," Violet said. "Let Clem take care of it."

"Don't you think that best?" Daisy looked at her husband.

"Levi and I won't get a wink of sleep for wondering what's happening. We might as well go see. I doubt if Clem will come back here tonight and tell us anything."

"But it's dark, and I hate to think of you being out there all night." Daisy turned her worried face to her husband.

Noah went to his wife's side. "Levi and I will be just fine. It's nicer weather than when we go hunting all night in the fall. Besides, this will free up an extra bed for Mrs. Ramsey and her daughter."

"I thought they could share the bedroom with Violet." Daisy held onto Noah's arm.

Levi shook his head. "I'd have slept in the barn tonight and let them have my bed, but Noah's right. I'd like to know what's happening. If Orin refuses to leave, I'll watch Orin and send Noah into Boone for the sheriff. The three of us will see justice done. There's no way I'm going to let Orin get away with this."

"It could wait until morning." Like Daisy, Anna hated to see Levi leave in the night.

Levi gave her the special look he only had for her. "I'll just worry the night through. Like Noah said, it's best to go on now."

"So we can worry the night through instead." Daisy said the words in Anna's mind.

"Trust God to keep us safe." Levi looked at Daisy first, but then turned his gaze on Anna. "He's in control and wants the best for us all."

"Sometimes I wish I had your faith, Levi." Violet's statement surprised Anna.

"You can," Levi told her. "Just ask Him to help you."

"Well, we'd best get going before it gets any later." Noah gave his wife a kiss on the cheek. "Pack us something to eat, and don't worry if we don't make it back tomorrow. I'll go get the lanterns from the barn."

Levi put Ellie down on the bed in the living area where it looked like he slept. He and Noah had just ridden away when she awoke. She looked around confused.

Anna pulled her close. "It's okay, darling. We're visiting with Levi's family for a while."

"Daddy?"

"Levi and his brother had to go out, but he'll be back soon." And she prayed unharmed.

Levi and Noah rode along in silence. They went at a much slower pace than Levi would have liked, but they had to pick their way along the trail in the dim light of the lanterns. The clear night had a half-moon, but the dense forest allowed little of its light in.

In the quiet, his mind ran back to Anna. He first felt such joy the moment he saw her ride up, knowing she'd come to him. But, the realization that something must be terribly wrong had turned the joy into worry.

He imagined her back at the cabin. Had she and Ellie already eaten? Would she sleep well in his bed tonight? That thought brought emotions he hadn't expected. He'd known for a long time that he loved Anna, but he hadn't realized the depth of that love until now.

*Lord, help us to honor Thee with our love. Don't
let carnal feelings overcome the purity of what I feel for
Anna. Orchestrate good to come from this situation with
Orin, and above all, Thy will be done. Amen.*

With the slowness of the trip, they didn't make it
to Anna's cabin until after sunrise. Clem came from the
barn with a milk bucket in his hand. He walked up to
them as they dismounted and looked down at the milk.
"The cow needed takin' ceer of. Orin's fixin' breakfast,
and he'll have the coffee ready. Come on in."

"What's he saying?" Levi asked.

Clem shook his head. "He's not listenin' to reason
and still says he's not stayin' at ar place when I marry
Violet."

Clem waited while Levi and Noah unsaddled the
horses. They both took their rifles to carry in with them.
Clem raised his eyebrows but didn't say anything.

"What're they doin' here?" Orin frowned.

"Well, you ain't listenin' to me, so maybe they can
talk some sense into that thick skull of yourn."

"You ain't welcome here if'n you thank you have
to be totin' a gun."

They set their rifles by the door. It would be easy
enough to grab them if needed.

"I'll pour us some coffee." Clem moved to get the
cups.

Levi shut his eyes for a moment. Seeing Orin's
clumsy movements where Anna should be and Clem

pouring his coffee instead of her didn't sit well with him.

"Don't thank you're goin' talk me outa this," Orin said. "Clem tried, and I ain't budgin'."

Levi looked at the man. "Do you believe in God?"

Orin seemed taken aback. "Yeah, I do. I ain't crazy 'bout religion like some I know, but I believe in God. Was even baptized back when I wuz a youngin'."

"Do you think God is happy with what you've done here, kicking a widow and her young daughter out of their home?"

Orin scratched his head. "I hain't rightly thought about hit."

Levi pressed on. "In the Bible, James says to take care of the widows and orphans, and Anna is both. Psalms tells us to "defend the poor and fatherless" do justice to the afflicted and needy. Do you think you're doing justice?"

"Hit ain't right for Clem to kick me out either."

"Hey, wait just a minute here," Clem piped in. "I hain't kicked you out. It's your place just as much as it is mine. Besides, it wuz your idee for us to find wives anyways."

"Well, I thought I'd marry first, me bein' the oldest and all. And I had no idee that you'd marry a squawkin' blue jay that never shuts up."

Levi tried to contain his grin over Orin's description of Violet. At least Orin seemed to be listening to what they had to say.

"Violet's not like a blue jay." Clem almost looked as if he didn't know whether to be insulted or amused. "She looks more like a cardinal to me."

"Red bird's too quiet fer her," Orin muttered. "I ain't livin' with Violent, and that's all thar is to hit."

"Violet," Clem corrected. "Her name's Violet, like the flower."

"Should have named her 'Thorn,' 'cause she'll be a thorn in our sides fer sure."

"We're getting off the subject here." Levi didn't want to listen to the brothers argue about Violet. "You need to let Anna have her place back."

"No, Violet is the subject. She's why I'm stayin' put right here. I told Mrs. Ramsey she could stay here and marry me. Hit wuz her choice to leave."

Levi tried to control his frustration with the man. "If you ever get married and have a daughter, would you want her to marry some man who tried to force her into marriage the way you're doing to Anna?"

"You can talk until yo're blue in the face, but I ain't livin' with no violent woman." The twinkle in Orin's eyes told Levi the man knew exactly what he'd said.

Clem threw up his hands. "See they's no reasonin' with him. He's not budgin' any more'n the stubbornest of mules stuck in a quicksand bog."

"What if I bought you a corner of land off Noah's property and helped you build a cabin?" Levi understood they were going to have to take a different approach with Orin.

Orin looked at him quizzically. "You'd do that?"

"Yes, if it would get Anna back her farm."

"Hang on thar jist a minute," Clem interrupted. "We got plenty of land with ar place. He can jist build his cabin on some of hit and be closer to me. That way we could help each other out."

"Might still be too close to that woman." Orin's tone of voice had softened to one of humor, however.

Clem huffed. "You can build it acres away from the cabin. In fact, you can have the cabin, and I'll build a new one for me and Violet if'n you want. We're gettin' married Sunday after next. I want you to be thar."

Orin looked at Levi. "Can ya'll have the new cabin built by then?"

"We should at least have most of it done. You can camp out at it if it's not completely finished."

He nodded. "Okay then. I reckon Mrs. Ramsey can move on back. I'll stay with Clem until the weddin', and we'll figure out between us who will be stayin' in which."

"We're goin' to take a quick nap in the barn before we head back," Noah told him.

Levi and Noah were both so tired they camped out part of the night and made it back to the farm at daylight. Anna came running to him, and his arms went around her immediately. She didn't protest or pull away.

"What happened?" she finally asked. It seemed as if her farm was less important than his safe return.

"Levi talked the man into giving you back your place," Noah answered.

"Without a fight?" she asked.

"Just a verbal one." Levi laughed.

"Come on." She took him by the hand. "You can tell me all about it over breakfast."

Ellie came running to him and threw herself in his arms. "Daddy!" He never tired of hearing her say that.

"You really are special to that girl," Daisy said. "She and Iris have been inseparable until you come in, and Ellie immediately leaves her newfound friend for her 'daddy.'"

Levi's heart wanted to burst with pride and joy. Dare he say it? "I'd love to be her real daddy." He looked at Anna.

A pretty blush came to her face, but she gave a tentative smile. "You're Ellie's and my hero."

"Well, that sounds like I've climbed quite a few notches in your estimation. I can remember a time when you didn't ever want to see me again."

Her face became redder. "We'll talk more about it later."

What did that mean? Had she rethought agreeing to him courting her and decided they needed to part? But with that statement about him being her hero, could she possibly want him as her husband? No, she'd made the stipulation they move slowly, and he was trying, despite how hard he found it to be.

That night, Levi slept in the barn, despite Anna's protests. He'd assured her that, as tired as he felt, he would sleep fine out there, and he did.

The next morning, they left early for her place. Orin would do the morning milking and be gone by the time they got there, but they would need to do the evening milking.

Levi could tell both Anna and Ellie were excited to be going home, but he could have kept them with him indefinitely. "I wish you would stay until after Violet's wedding."

"You said Orin was leaving today, and I'll need to do the chores at the farm." She sighed. "I wish I hadn't even told Violet I'd come. I'm not part of the family."

Oh, but he wished she were. "Since I'm courting you, you're close enough to family."

She didn't look amused. "Don't use that against me."

"I'm not. I'm just looking forward to seeing you again in about a week. If you really don't want to go, however, I'll give everyone your regrets."

He'd told Noah he might not be back until the wedding, but that would depend on Anna. He'd sleep in the barn if she invited him, but he didn't want to keep forcing himself on her.

"I'm sorry. I didn't mean to be so surly with you. No, I told Violet and Daisy I would come, and I will." She gave him a tentative smile. "I'm looking forward to seeing you in about a week, too."

"That makes me feel better." He knew his grin had nothing tentative about it. "Do you need to take a break?" She seemed uncomfortable on the horse.

"No, thank you. I'm all right for a while longer. I'll let you know when I need one."

"Have you ridden much?"

She laughed. "No, I haven't, and I'm sure it shows. I'm just glad you have Ellie riding in front of you this time. I can still feel some soreness from our last ride."

"I'm proud of you for coming to me and finding your way."

"Where else did I have to go?"

He didn't like the sound of that. "You could have gone into Boone and spoken with the sheriff."

"I didn't think of that, and it would have been closer. I just knew if I could get to you, you would take care of us and the situation."

"I'm glad. I want to always be there for you." Did she understand the underlying meaning of that statement?

Chapter Seventeen: Violet's Wedding

Every time Levi tried to ask Anna what she meant by her statement of explaining about not wanting to see him before, she avoided the issue. If she couldn't divert the subject, she'd say, "I'm not ready to talk about it yet, and I shouldn't have mentioned it. Please give me some more time." If their relationship did nothing else, it would have to teach him patience.

Ellie had napped some along the way, but she sat wide awake when the cabin came in sight. "Home."
"Yes, we're home now," Anna told her. They were all ready to be off the horses.
Levi hurried around to do the chores, while Anna made a quick supper for them. They'd already eaten all the food Daisy had sent along.
She fried cornbread fritters and put a fried egg on top of it. Levi had never eaten this before, but it tasted delicious. He ate four of them.

"It's a good thing Orin left us some eggs." Anna chuckled, but he could tell she liked that he'd eaten so much.

"You'll stay the night?"

He nodded. "Yes, I'll sleep in the barn."

"You're welcome to stay in the cabin. You can either sleep with Ellie or have the bed in here."

"I'd better not, although I'd love to do that. Orin or Clem might come around, and it would be better if they found me in the barn and not in the house."

"Thank you for trying to protect my reputation."

"I always want to do what's best for you and put you first, however much they go against my desires, and what I'd really like to do."

"Now you're being mischievous." She didn't laugh, but her eyes did.

Anna had pancakes ready when he brought in the milk the next morning. "Ellie's not up yet, but let's eat ours while they're warm. I'll save hers."

Levi smiled. He didn't get to sit at the table and eat breakfast with just the two of them often.

"I've been thinking," Anna began. "It would take you two or three days of traveling time to get to your place and then come back to take me to the wedding. That would only leave you two days there. Why don't you just stay here until after the wedding and avoid all that traveling? If you don't have the clothes to wear, we could go in on Saturday and get you some in Boone."

"I'll have to go help the men build Orin a new cabin. Noah asked some others he knew to help so we can get it done faster. But I actually brought my church clothes with me for the wedding, although they'll probably need ironing before I wear them."

"Good. I need to do some laundry today. Give me your clothes, and I'll iron everything tomorrow. You will come back here to stay in the evenings, won't you?"

"I'll see how things go and how far away the site Orin picked out is. Don't worry about it if I don't make it back, but I'll try. I'd rather be here."

The week went by much too quickly for Levi, because he'd need to go back to Noah's after the wedding. He and the men had gotten the cabin built. The furnishings would be up to Orin. There were enough men to help that he'd been able to leave early enough to get back to Anna's by dark. She always had him a supper plate fixed and waiting for him.

He and Anna got up early Sunday morning to get the chores done and get ready to leave. They'd need to get back tonight in time to milk, but it would be much later than usual. He set out two lanterns to take with them, because he didn't know for sure how late the wedding would run.

He put on his church clothes and walked around with Ellie outside while Anna finished getting ready. When she walked out, she nearly took his breath.

"You look lovely." Quite an understatement, but the best he could do in his speechless state.

She looked down at the skirt of her dress. "It's the pale blue fabric you gave me. I've been saving it for a special occasion."

"I should have bought you some others."

She laughed. "You bought me enough to make three dresses. That's plenty, extravagant really."

"You deserve a wardrobe full." Didn't she know he didn't consider anything extravagant where she and Ellie were concerned?

"You're a puzzling man."

"How so?" He helped her into the wagon and handed Ellie up.

"I've never met a man so giving or considerate. You continually surprise me."

"That's because you've never met a man who's so in love with you."

She turned her head and muttered something he couldn't quite hear. It sounded like "too good to be true."

Was he rushing things again? But she needed to know how he felt.

He regretted his comment even more as he drove the wagon toward Boone. Anna sat quietly and deep in thought, so he focused on entertaining Ellie. She'd point to something and say, "What's dat?" He would tell her and she'd repeat it, however, she knew most of the words already. Soon he turned the game around and asked her what things were.

Even with stopping to eat the dinner Anna had packed, they got to the church in plenty of time. Clem and Violet had scheduled their wedding for two o'clock, as early as they could and still give people time to eat after church.

More came than Levi expected, but then he remembered Noah saying people would turn out for weddings and funerals, and more people were free on a Sunday afternoon. Still, the church didn't quite fill.

Orin hung his head and muttered an apology to Anna. "I'm sorry about what I done. I guess hit wuzn't a very neighborly thang to do."

"No, it wasn't," Anna said, "but I accept your apology."

He nodded and walked off with his shoulders slumped. "This here's a sad day for me," he mumbled.

"You know, I can see Orin's point about this being a sad day for him."

"Levi! I can't believe you said that." But she laughed and looked thoroughly amused. He loved to hear her laugh.

Violet looked the prettiest he'd ever seen her as she walked down the aisle in a pale yellow dress, but no one could outshine Anna. Others thought so, too, by the stares of some of the single men.

Violet had asked Pansy, her sister who was ten months younger, to be her maid of honor, along with

Daisy who was the matron of honor. Clem had chosen Orin to be his best man, and Noah was also part of the wedding party, so he could escort Daisy.

Orin couldn't take his eyes off Pansy, but she was so shy, she didn't know how to act. Levi grinned in amusement and saw Anna do the same. Now this could be an interesting development. From what little Levi had seen of Pansy, Orin couldn't complain about her talking too much.

During the ceremony, Levi watched Anna become emotional. Did all women have tears well up in their eyes during a wedding? He didn't think that could be the cause, because Anna and Violet had never become close. No, this must be something more personal. Did it bring back bad memories of her own wedding and how that turned out, or did she dream of another wedding and a fulfilling marriage? He hoped for the latter.

He reached over and picked up her hand to hold. She swallowed, gave him a weak smile, and squeezed his hand but didn't pull hers away. Good. She still accepted his support and comfort.

The preacher's wife had organized a simple reception with cookies and apple cider afterwards. Daisy sat with Ellie and Iris helping them with their food.

"Let's step outside for a minute," he told Anna.

"I'll just go tell Daisy where we'll be."

He watched her walk over to the table and whisper in Daisy's ear. Ellie had her full attention on Iris and didn't notice. He led Anna out back where they could see the creek in the distance.

"Were you upset during the wedding?"

She nodded. "A little."

"Care to talk about it?"

"I found myself wishing my first wedding and marriage had been different. I wish I'd married someone like you."

His heart did a funny little twist. "Does that mean you want to marry me?"

She didn't answer, so he tried another tactic. "You never did tell me what you were going to about pushing me away."

"I regret that now, but at the time, I thought it for the best. I'm glad you were persistent and never gave up."

Had he heard her correctly? Did she really say those words?

"What are you saying, Anna?" He needed to be sure.

"You told me today that I'd never met a man as much in love with me as you are. Well, you're my first real love."

It took a moment for the words to sink in. He'd waited so long to hear them that now they'd come, he could hardly believe his ears.

He pulled her into his arms. "Oh, darling, you've made me a very happy man."

He moved back a few inches so he could see her face. "Does that mean that you will marry me?"

"If that's a proposal, then the answer is 'Yes.'"

"Oh, darling!" That's all he got out before his lips took hers. Never had he imagined the charge that ran through his whole body. Never had he known there could be such ecstasy. He could have stayed just like that forever if he hadn't needed more air. "When?" It came out as a gasp.

"When would you like?" Her voice trembled a little and she still held on to him for support, but he didn't mind. No he didn't mind at all. "What about today?"

He didn't know if she teased, if her brain had been scrambled as much as his from that kiss, or if she spoke in all seriousness. "No, not today." A coherent thought finally took hold. "You deserve a wedding day all your own and not at the tail end of Violet's. What about tomorrow?"

She stepped back. "You're serious?"

"And you weren't?" His heart nearly stopped at the thought she might have just been teasing all along.

"Tomorrow it is, but how will we arrange it. Where will we stay, and what about Ellie?"

"Come on." He led her toward the church. "I'll talk to the preacher and the family, and we'll see what works best."

Daisy immediately offered to take Ellie with her. "She and Iris will have a good time. They both need a playmate."

He and Anna pulled Ellie aside to tell her. "You know how you always call me 'Daddy,'" Levi said. "How would you like for me to be your real daddy, like Noah is Iris's real daddy?"

Her eyes lit up. "Oh, yes. Can you?"

"He can if he and I get married," Anna told her. "If we get married tomorrow, you can go stay with Iris for a week. Would you like that?"

Ellie gave a hesitant nod. "But I like staying with Daddy, too."

"We'll come get you next Monday," Levi told her, "and then the three of us will be together."

"Forever and ever?"

He smiled. "Yes. Forever and ever."

"Okay."

The pastor's wife invited Anna and Ellie to stay at her house overnight. Levi would get a room in the boarding house. He asked Orin to go by and milk Anna's cow, and he said he would. Noah would take his family home to do chores and come back tomorrow. They set the wedding for one o'clock.

"I'm going to wear this suit tomorrow," he told Anna. "I wish the store had ready-to-wear for women, but I don't think they do."

"I'm fine with wearing this dress. I love the material and the fact that you chose it. Do you mind me wearing the same dress I wore today?"

"Not at all. It looks beautiful on you, and I know it's better made than anything you could buy if they did have ready-made dresses."

Her eyes took on a mischievous gleam he'd never seen before. "I'd much rather marry you tomorrow than to wait for a new dress."

He laughed at her boldness. He couldn't wait to get to know this new Anna who wasn't afraid of marrying him.

Despite the strange room and unfamiliar bed, Ellie went to sleep immediately. Of course, she hadn't had her nap today either. It took Anna much longer. She lay there in her borrowed nightgown thinking of all that had happened since she'd come to the mountains.

She could scarce believe she'd be getting married again tomorrow. The thought scared her to the core until she reminded herself she'd be marrying Levi. He had a way of making everything all right for her. She couldn't figure out if he tried hard to please her or if he just had a caring nature, but it didn't matter. Either way, she felt cherished.

She almost shook her head at how hard she'd fought her feelings for him. She'd been in love with the man for a long time, but she'd refused to recognize it and tried to push him away. But the stubborn man wouldn't stay gone for long. She thanked God for that. She thanked God for bringing Levi West into her life.

She awoke the next morning to clouds and haze, common for a mountain morning, but it burned off before dinnertime, and the afternoon turned bright and sunny. She'd tried to tell Levi it was considered bad luck for the groom to see the bride on their wedding day before she walked down the aisle, but he'd laughed at her.

"I don't believe in luck. I believe in God's blessings," he said. "Besides, I would be miserable indeed if I had to be this close to you and couldn't see you for more than half a day."

"You managed to be close to me without seeing me when you came to my cabin in secret and slept in the barn," she told him.

"Oh, I saw you – from afar – and I was miserable at having to stay away from your sight."

"I'm sorry." Sorry because they'd lost too much time because of her foolishness.

"Don't be." His eyes took on that look she'd learned meant he planned to tease. "I'll let you make it all up to me as soon as the preacher announces us husband and wife."

At one time she would have blushed, but now she liked his teasing. When she admitted her true feelings for him, she'd realized how deeply she'd fallen in love. And, remarkably, he seemed to be just as madly in love with her.

He came to pick her up after breakfast. Reverend Greene had offered for him and his wife to keep Ellie for them, but Levi wanted her with them, since she'd be leaving with Daisy that afternoon. His concern for Ellie also endeared him to Anna. She had no doubt that he already loved the child as his own daughter.

"I'm glad you insisted we spend the morning together," Anna told him as they walked back toward Reverend Greene's house for dinner. "It would have been a long morning of waiting otherwise."

He picked up her hand and kissed it. "For me, too. I can't wait for you to become my wife."

"Me, too, Daddy?" Ellie asked.

Levi picked Ellie up and swung her around. "I'll be your daddy or papa, and you'll be my daughter." He ended the maneuver with Ellie cackling with laughter, but he kept her in his arms. "That reminds me. What do you think of me adopting Ellie, so she'll be mine legally, too?"

"I think that's a fine idea. I would hate for something to happen to me and some of Elbert's relatives I never knew about come out of the woodwork and try to take her from you."

Levi turned a bit pale. "I pray nothing's going to happen to you, but I'd like to be completely truthful when I say she's my daughter."

Anna just picked at her food, much too restless to eat, but Levi didn't seem to have that problem. She needed to freshen up, too, before she went to the church.

"I'll take Ellie and go on to the church with Reverend Greene. You and Mrs. Greene can come along when you're ready." Levi must have read her mind.

"You have yourself a thoughtful, considerate man there, Anna," Mrs. Greene said. "But come on, now, let's go fix your hair. We don't want to leave a good man like that waiting for long."

Mrs. Greene put her hair up and wove some honeysuckle through it. Anna liked the scent. When she'd finished, she handed Anna a bouquet of roses and wildflowers. Anna raised her eyebrows to question where they came from. "Levi told me to make it for you." Mrs. Greene said.

Noah had agreed to walk her down the aisle to Levi. Since she'd been married before, she chose not to have attendants. When she stepped through the doors and took his arm, the aroma of flowers caressed her. Every window sill, every table, and seemingly the whole church had been filled with flowers.

Her eyes locked on Levi's, and when he smiled, she knew he'd had this done. Her eyes never left his as she walked toward him. Maybe it was the magic of so many flowers, or maybe it was the love she saw in

Levi's eyes, but suddenly the wedding took on a dream-like quality and became her fantasy wedding. Without a doubt, she knew everything would be just fine.

As soon as the ceremony ended and they'd greeted everyone, Levi and she said good-bye to Ellie and his family and then headed toward the cabin. If they hurried, they could be home by dark.

"I'll go change clothes and fix us a bite to eat while you milk," she told him when he brought the wagon to a halt in the backyard of the cabin.

"Not so fast." He secured the reins to the wagon, jumped down, scooped her up, and carried her into the house.

"What are you doing?" she asked through her laughter.

"Carrying my new bride over the threshold."

She started to protest, but clamped her mouth shut instead. She liked the feel of being in his arms too much.

When they were inside, he sat her down, kissed her thoroughly, and started outside to unhitch the wagon and milk. "I'd love some more of those corn fritters with eggs," he threw back over his shoulders. "A quick supper will be good."

She heard him whistling as he went about his chores and smiled. Fritters and eggs it would be.

She awoke in her own bedroom to find Levi by her side watching her. She moved to put her head on his shoulder, and he kissed her forehead. "How do you feel, sweetheart?"

She couldn't possibly find the words to tell him how she felt. "Overwhelmed with love." That would have to do.

"Good." He rubbed the hair away from her face. "I want you to feel loved, although you could never really know how much love I have for you. However, I'll have a lifetime to try to show you."

She stroked his cheek. "I have a pretty good idea. You show me in so many ways, and I also love you too much for words. You're the husband I've dreamed of for years and the man I've been searching for all my adult life. In fact, the reality of being your wife is better than any dream I ever had. I never imagined loving could be this wonderful. I hate you had that mishap on the mountain and sliced your leg to bring us together, but I wouldn't take it back if it meant we'd never meet. "

"That wasn't a mishap, darling. That was God directing our paths."

He wrapped her in his arms and gave her a kiss that made her forget words even existed. She looked forward to a lifetime of this.

For more information about

Janice Cole Hopkins

Web page: www.JaniceColeHopkins.blogspot.com

Email: wandrnlady@aol.com

Twitter: @J_C_Hopkins

Facebook: www.facebook.com/JaniceColeHopkins
(Please like this author's page)

If you enjoyed the book, please leave a review on Amazon and/or similar sites to let others know. This is the best way to say "Thank you" to an author.

All the author's profits go to a scholarship fund for missionary children.

51788978R00136

Made in the USA
Middletown, DE
04 July 2019